Liv bristled. "I don't need someone to protect me."

"No one can watch their own back," Hawkeye said. "As a member of the armed forces, I know what it means to trust the guys behind me."

"Who did you have in mind?"

He smiled. "Me."

A thrill of something she hadn't felt in a long time—if she didn't count the kiss—rippled through Liv. Taking on Hawkeye could prove to be a big mistake in more ways than one. "What choice do I have?"

"None," Hawkeye said, his tone firm and final.

For however long it took to find her father's murderer and stop this insanity going on in her community, she was stuck with Hawkeye. And despite her initial resistance, she had to admit to herself she might just need him.

HOT ZONE

New York Times Bestselling Author
ELLE JAMES

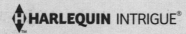

This book is dedicated to my daughters, who chose to give back to their country by joining the military. Thank you for following in your mother's footsteps! Love you both so much!

ISBN-13: 978-0-373-75679-7

Hot Zone

Copyright © 2017 by Mary Jernigan

Recycling programs for this product may not exist in your area.

Printed in U.S.A.

www.Harlequin.com

Elle James, a *New York Times* bestselling author, started writing when her sister challenged her to write a romance novel. She has managed a full-time job and raised three wonderful children, and she and her husband even tried ranching exotic birds (ostriches, emus and rheas). Ask her, and she'll tell you what it's like to go toe-to-toe with an angry 350-pound bird! Elle loves to hear from fans at ellejames@earthlink.net or ellejames.com.

Visit the Author Profile page at Harlequin.com for more titles.

CAST OF CHARACTERS

Trace "Hawkeye" Walsh—US Army Airborne Ranger and expert sniper, on loan to the Department of Homeland Security for Task Force Safe Haven, a special group of military men.

Olivia "Liv" Dawson—Returns to Grizzly Pass to take over the running of the family ranch when her father dies in a ranching accident.

Kevin Garner—Agent with the Department of Homeland Security in charge of Task Force Safe Haven.

Jon "Ghost" Caspar—US Navy SEAL on loan to the Department of Homeland Security for Task Force Safe Haven.

Max "Caveman" Decker—US Army DELTA Force soldier on loan to the Department of Homeland Security for Task Force Safe Haven.

Rex "T-Rex" Trainor—US Marine on loan to the Department of Homeland Security for Task Force Safe Haven.

Ernie Martin—Rancher angry about cessation of government subsidies on his Angora goat ranching business.

Bryson Rausch—Formerly the wealthiest resident of Grizzly Pass, who lost a great deal of money in the stock market, but still owns much of Grizzly Pass.

Don Sweeney—Works at the feed store, dishonorably discharged from the military.

CJ Running Bear—Ernie Martin's stepson. Native American teen trying to help feed his mother and siblings.

Chapter One

Trace "Hawkeye" Walsh checked the coordinates he'd been given by Transcontinental Pipeline Inspection, Inc., and glanced down at the display on the four-wheeler's built-in GPS guidance device. He'd arrived at checkpoint number four. He switched off the engine, climbed off the ATV and unfolded the contour map across the seat.

As with the first three checkpoints, he wasn't exactly sure what he was looking for at the location. He wasn't a pipeline inspector, and he didn't have the tools and devices used by one, but he scanned the area anyway.

Tracing his finger along the line drawn in pencil across the page, he paused. He should be getting close to the point at which RJ Khalig had been murdered. Based on the tight contour lines on the map, he would find the spot over the top of the next ridgeline and down in the valley.

Hawkeye glanced upward. Treacherous terrain had slowed him down. In order to reach some of the points on the map, he'd had to follow old mining trails and bypass canyons. He shrugged. It wasn't a war zone, he wasn't fighting the Taliban or ISIS, and it beat the hell out of being in an office job any day of the week.

That morning, his temporary boss, Kevin Garner, had given him the assignment of following the pipeline through some of the most rugged terrain he'd ever been in, even considering the foothills of Afghanistan. He was game. If he had to be working with the Department of Homeland Security in the Beartooth Mountains of Wyoming, he was happy to be out in the backwoods, rather than chasing wild geese, empty leads and the unhappy residents of the tiny town of Grizzly Pass.

In the two weeks he'd been in the small town of Grizzly Pass, they'd had two murders, a busload of kids taken hostage and two people hunted down like wild game. When he'd agreed to the assignment, he'd been looking forward to some fresh mountain air and a slowdown to his normal combat-heavy assignments. He needed the time to determine whether or not he would stay the full twenty years to retirement in the US Army Rangers or get out and dare to try something different.

Two gunshot and multiple shrapnel wounds, one broken arm, a couple of concussions and six near-fatal misses started to wear on a body and soul. In the last battle he'd been a part of, his best friend hadn't been as lucky. The gunshot wound had been nothing compared to the violent explosion Mac had been smack-dab in the middle of. Yeah, Hawkeye had lost his best friend and battle buddy, a man who'd had his back since they'd been rangers in training.

Without Mac, he wasn't sure he wanted to continue to deploy to the most godforsaken, war-torn countries in the world. He wasn't sure he'd survive. And maybe that wasn't a bad thing. At least he'd die like Mac, defending his country.

He'd hoped this temporary assignment would give him the opportunity to think about his next steps in life. Should he continue his military career? His enlistment was up in a month. He had to decide whether to reenlist or get out.

So far, since he'd been in Grizzly Pass, he

hadn't had the time to ponder his future. Hell, he'd already been in a shoot-out and had to rescue one of his new team members. For a place with such a small population, it was a hot zone of trouble. No wonder Garner had requested combat veterans to assist him in figuring out what the hell was going on.

Thankfully, today was just a fact-finding mission. He was to traverse the line Khalig had been inspecting when he'd met with his untimely demise. He was to look for any clues as to why someone would have paid Wayne Batson to assassinate him. Since Batson was dead, they couldn't ask him. And he hadn't been forthcoming with a name before he took his final breath.

Which meant whoever had hired him was still out there, having gotten away with murder.

Hawkeye double-checked the map, oriented with the antique compass his grandfather had given him when he'd joined the army and cross-checked with the GPS. Sure of his directions, he folded the map, pocketed his compass, climbed onto the ATV and took off.

At the top of the ridge, he paused and glanced around, looking for other vehicles or people on the opposite ridge. He didn't want to get caught like Khalig at the bottom of the valley with a sniper itching to pick him off. Out of the corner of his eye, he detected movement in the valley below.

A man squatted beside another four-wheeler. He had something in his hands and seemed to be burying it in the dirt.

Hawkeye goosed the throttle, sending his four-wheeler over the edge, descending the winding trail.

The man at the bottom glanced up. When he spotted Hawkeye descending the trail on the side of the hill, he dropped what he'd been holding, leaped onto his ATV and raced up an old mining road on the other side of the ridge.

Hopping off the trail, Hawkeye took the more direct route to the bottom, bouncing over large rock stumps and fallen branches of weathered trees. By the time Hawkeye arrived at the base, the man who'd sped away was already halfway up the hill in front of him.

Hawkeye paused long enough to look at what the man had dropped, and his blood ran cold. A stick of dynamite jutted out of the ground with a long fuse coiled in the dirt beside it.

Thumbing the throttle lever, Hawkeye zoomed after the disappearing rider, who had apparently been about to sabotage the oil pipeline. Had he succeeded, he would have had the entire state in an uproar over the spillage and damage to the environment.

Not to mention, he might be the key to who had contracted Batson to kill Khalig.

At the top of the hill where the mining road wrapped around the side of a bluff, Hawkeye slowed in case the pursued had stopped to attack his pursuer.

Easing around the corner, he noted the path was clear and spied the rider heading down a trail Hawkeye could see from his vantage point would lead back to a dirt road and ultimately to the highway. With as much of a lead as he had, Dynamite Man could conceivably reach the highway and get away before Hawkeye caught up.

Hawkeye refused to let the guy off the hook. Goosing the accelerator, he shot forward and hurtled down the narrow mining road to the base of the mountain. At several points along the path, he skidded sideways, the rear wheels of the four-wheeler sliding dangerously close to the edge of deadly drop-offs. But he didn't slow his descent, pushing his speed faster than was prudent on the rugged terrain.

By the time he reached the bottom of the mountain, Hawkeye was within fifty yards of the man on the other ATV. His quarry wouldn't have enough time to ditch his four-wheeler for another vehicle.

Hawkeye followed the dirt road, occasionally losing sight of the rider in front of him. Eventually, between the trees and bushes, he caught glimpses of the highway ahead. When he broke free into a rare patch of open terrain, he spied the man on the track ahead, about to hit the highway's pavement.

"I'LL BE DAMNED if I sell Stone Oak Ranch to Bryson Rausch. My father would roll over in his grave." At the thought of her father lying in his grave next to her mother, Olivia Dawson's heart clenched in her chest. Her eyes stung, but anger kept her from shedding another tear.

"You said you couldn't live at the ranch. Not since your father died." Abe Masterson, the Stone Oak Ranch foreman for the past twenty years, turned onto the highway headed toward home.

Liv's throat tightened. Home. She'd wanted to come home since she graduated from college three years ago. But her father had insisted she try city living before she decided whether or not she wanted to come back to the hard work and solitary life of a rancher.

For the three years since she'd left college with a shiny new degree, she'd worked her way up the corporate ladder to a management position. Eight people reported directly to her. She was responsible for their output and their well-being. She'd promised her father she'd give it five years. But that had all changed in the space of one second.

The second her father died in a freak horse-back-riding accident six days earlier.

Liv had gotten the word in the middle of the night in Seattle, had hopped into her car and had driven all the way to Grizzly Pass, Wyoming. No amount of hurrying back to her home would have been fast enough to have allowed her to say goodbye to her father.

By the time Abe had found him, he'd been dead for a couple of hours. The coroner estimated the fall had killed him instantly, when he'd struck his head on a rock.

Liv would have given anything to have talked to him one last time. She hadn't spoken to him for over a week before his death. The last time had been on the telephone and had ended in anger. She had wanted to end her time in Seattle and come home. Her father had insisted she finish out her five years.

I'm not going to get married to a city boy. What use would he be on a ranch, anyway? she'd argued.

You don't know where love will take you. Give it a chance, he'd argued right back. *Have you been dating?*

No, Dad. I intimidate most men. They like their women soft and wimpy. I can't do that. It's not me.

Sweetheart, her father had said. *You have to open your heart. Love hits you when you least expect it. Besides, I want to live to see my grandchildren.*

Her throat tightening, Liv shook her head. Her father would never know his grandchildren, and they'd never know the great man he was. The tears welled and threatened to slip out the corners of her eyes.

"If you sell to Rausch, you can be done with ranching and get on with your life. You won't have to stay around, being constantly reminded of your father."

"Maybe I want to be reminded. Maybe I was being too rash when I said I couldn't be around the ranch because it brought back too many painfully happy memories of me and Dad." She sniffed, angry that she wasn't doing a very good job of holding herself together.

"What did Rausch offer you?"

Liv wiped her eyes with her sleeve and swallowed the lump in her throat before she could force words out. "A quarter of what the ranch is worth. A quarter!" She laughed, the sound ending in a sob. "I'll die herding cattle before I sell to that man."

"Yeah, well, you could die a lot sooner if you go like your father."

Liv clenched her fist in her lap. "It's physically demanding, ranching in the foothills of the Beartooth Mountains. Falling off your horse and hitting your head on a rock could happen to anyone around here." She shot a glance at Abe. "Right?"

He nodded, his voice dropping to little more than a whisper. "Yeah, but I would bet my best rodeo buckle your father had some help falling off that horse."

"What do you mean?"

"Just that we'd had some trouble on the ranch, leading up to that day."

"Trouble?"

Abe shrugged. "There've been a whole lot of strange things going on in Grizzly Pass in the past couple months."

"Dad never said a word."

"He didn't want to worry you."

Liv snorted and then sniffed. He was a little late on that account. She swiveled in her seat, directing her attention to the older man. "Tell me."

"You know about the kids on the hijacked bus, right?"

She nodded. "I heard about it on the national news. I couldn't believe the Vanderses went off the deep end. But what does that have to do with my father and the ranch?"

Abe lifted a hand and scratched his wiry brown hair with streaks of silver dominating his temples. "That's only part of the problem. I hear there's a group called Free America stirring up trouble."

"What kind of trouble?"

"Nothing anyone can put a finger on, but rumor has it they're meeting regularly, training in combat tactics."

"Doesn't the local law enforcement have a handle on them?"

Abe shook his head. "No one on the inside

is owning up to being a part of it, and folks on the outside are only guessing. It's breeding a whole lot of distrust among the locals."

"So they're training for combat. People have a right to protect themselves." She didn't like that it was splitting a once close-knit community.

"Yeah, but what if they put that combat training to use and try to take over the government?"

Liv smiled and leaned back in her seat. "They'd have to have a lot more people than the population of Grizzly Pass to take over the government."

"Maybe so, but they could do a lot of damage and terrorize a community if they tried anything locally. Just look at the trouble Vanders and his boys stirred up when they killed a bus driver and threatened to bury a bunch of little kids in one of the old mines."

"You have a point." Liv chewed on her lower lip, her brows drawing together. She could only imagine the horror those children had to face and the families standing by, praying for their release. "We used to be a caring, cohesive community. We had semiannual picnics where everyone came out and visited with each other. What's happening?"

"With the shutdown of the pipeline, a lot of folks are out of work. The government upped the fees for grazing cattle on federal land and there isn't much more than ranching in this area. People are moving to the cities, looking for work. Others are holding on by their fingernails."

Her heart ached for her hometown. "I didn't realize it was that bad."

"Yeah, I almost think you need to take Rausch's offer and get out of here while you can."

Her lips firmed into a thin line. "He was insulting, acting like I didn't know the business end of a horse. Hell, he doesn't know the first thing about ranching."

"Which leads me to wonder—"

Something flashed in front of the speeding truck. A rider on a four-wheeler.

Abe jerked the steering wheel to avoid hitting him and sent the truck careening over the shoulder of the road, down a steep slope, crashing into bushes and bumping over huge rocks.

Despite the safety belt across her chest, Liv was tossed about like a shaken rag doll.

"Hold on!" Abe cried out.

With a death grip on the armrest, Liv braced herself.

The truck slammed into a tree.

Liv was thrown forward, hitting her head on the dash. For a moment gray haze and sparkling stars swam in her vision.

A groan from the man next to her brought her out of the fog and back to the front seat of the pickup. She blinked several times and turned her head.

A sharp stab of pain slashed through her forehead and warm thick liquid dripped from her forehead into her eyes. She wiped the fluid away only to discover it was blood. Her blood.

Another moan took her mind off her own injuries.

She blinked to clear her vision and noticed Abe hunched over the steering wheel, the front of the truck pushed into the cab pressing in around his legs.

The pungent scent of gasoline stung her nostrils, sending warning signals through her stunned brain. "Abe?" She touched his shoulder.

His head lolled back, his eyes closed.

"Abe!" Liv struggled with her seat belt, the

buckle refusing to release when she pressed the button. "Abe!" She gave up for a moment and shook her foreman. "We have to get out of the truck. I smell gas."

He moaned again, but his eyes fluttered open. "I can't move," he said, his voice weak. "I think my leg is broken."

"I don't care if both of your legs are broken—we have to get you out of the truck. Now!" She punched at her own safety belt, this time managing to disengage the locking mechanism. Flinging it aside, she reached for Abe's and released it. Then she pushed open her door and slid out of the front seat.

When her feet touched the ground, her knees buckled. She grabbed hold of the door and held on to steady herself. The scent of gasoline was so strong now it was overpowering, and smoke rose from beneath the crumpled hood.

Straightening, Liv willed herself to be strong and get her foreman out of the truck before the vehicle burst into flames. She'd already lost her father. Abe was the only family she had left. She'd be damned if she lost him, too.

With tears threatening, she staggered around the rear of the truck, her feet slipping on loose gravel and stones. When she tried to open the driver's door, it wouldn't budge.

She pounded on it, getting more desperate by the minute. "Abe, you have to help me. Unlock the door. I have to get you out."

Rather than dissipating, the cloud of smoke grew. The wind shifted, sending the smoke into Liv's face. "Damn it, Abe. Unlock the door!"

A loud click sounded and Liv pulled the door handle, willing it to open. It didn't.

Her eyes stinging and the smoke scratching at her throat with every breath she took, Liv realized she didn't have much time.

She braced her foot on the side panel of the truck and pulled hard on the door handle. Metal scraped on metal and the door budged, but hung, having been damaged when the truck wrapped around the tree.

Hands curled around her shoulders, lifted her off her feet and set her to the side.

Then a hulk of a man with broad shoulders, big hands and a strong back ripped the door open, grabbed Abe beneath the arms, hauled him out of the smoldering cab and carried him all of the way up the hill to the paved road.

Her tears falling in earnest now, Liv followed, stumbling over the uneven ground, dropping to her knees every other step. When she reached the top, she sagged to the ground beside Abe on the shoulder of the road. "Abe? Please tell me you're okay. Please."

With his eyes still closed, he moaned. Then he lifted his eyelids and opened his mouth. "I'm okay," he muttered. "But I think my leg's broken."

"Oh, jeez, Abe." She laughed, albeit shakily. "A leg we can get fixed. I'm just glad you're alive."

"Take a lot more than a tree to do me in." Abe grabbed her arm. "I'm sorry, Liv. If it's messed up, I won't be able to take care of the place until it's healed."

"Oh, for Pete's sake, Abe. Working for me is the last thing you should be worrying about. I'll manage fine on my own." She rested her hand on her foreman's shoulder, amazed that the man could worry about her when his face was gray with pain. "What's more important is getting you to a hospital." She glanced around, looking for the man who'd pulled Abe from the wreckage.

He stood on the pavement, waving at a passing truck.

The truck slowed to a stop, and her rescuer

rounded to the driver's door and spoke with the man behind the wheel. The driver pulled to the side of the road, got out and hurried down to where Liv waited with Abe.

"Jonah? That you?" Abe glanced up, shading his eyes from the sun.

"Yup." Jonah dropped to his haunches beside Abe. "How'd you end up in a ditch?"

Abe shook his head and winced. "A man on a four-wheeler darted out in front of me. I swerved to miss him." He nodded toward Liv. "You remember Olivia Dawson?"

Jonah squinted, staring across Abe to Liv. "I remember a much smaller version of the Dawson girl." He held out his hand. "Sorry to hear about your father's accident."

Liv took the man's hand, stunned that they were making introductions when Abe was in pain. "Thank you. Seems accidents are going around." Liv stared from Abe to Jonah's vehicle above. "Think between the three of us we could get Abe up to your truck? He won't admit it, but I'll bet he's hurting pretty badly."

"It's just a little sore," Abe countered and then grimaced.

Liv snorted. "Liar."

"We can get him up there," the stranger said.

"Yes, we can," Jonah agreed. "But should we? I could drive back to town and notify the fire department. They could have an ambulance out here in no time."

"I don't need an ambulance to get me to town." Abe tried to get up. The movement made him cry out and his face turn white. He sagged back against the ground.

"If you don't want an ambulance, then you'll have to put up with us jostling you around getting you up the hill," the stranger said.

"Better than being paraded through Grizzly Pass in the back of an ambulance." Abe gritted his teeth. "Everyone knows ambulances are for sick folk."

"Or injured people," Liv said. "And you have a major injury."

"Probably just a bruise. Give me a minute and I'll be up and running circles around all of you." Abe caught Liv's stare and sighed. "Okay, okay. I could use a hand getting up the hill."

The stranger shot a glance at Jonah. "Let's do this."

Jonah looped one of Abe's arms around his neck, bent and slid an arm beneath one of Abe's legs.

The stranger stepped between Liv and Abe,

draped one of Abe's arms over his shoulder and glanced across at Jonah. "On three." He slipped his hand beneath Abe.

Jonah nodded. "One. Two. Three."

They straightened as one.

Abe squeezed his eyes shut and groaned, all of the color draining from his face.

Liv wanted to help, but knew she'd only get in the way. The best thing she could do at that point was to open the truck door before they got there with Abe. She raced up the steep hill, her feet sliding in the gravel. When she reached the top, she flung open the door to the backseat of the truck cab and turned back to watch Abe's progression.

The two men struggled up the hill, being as careful as they could while slipping on loose pebbles.

Liv's glance took in her father's old farm truck, the front wrapped around the tree. Smoke filled the cab and flames shot up from the engine compartment. She was surprised either one of them had lived. If Abe hadn't slammed on his brakes as quickly as he had, the outcome would have been much worse.

Her gaze caught a glimpse of another vehicle

on the other side of the truck. A four-wheeler was parked a few feet away.

Anger surged inside Liv. She almost said something to the stranger about how he'd nearly killed two people because of his carelessness. One look at Abe's face made Liv bite down hard on her tongue to keep from yelling at the man who'd nearly caused a fatal accident. Once Abe was taken care of, she'd have words with the man.

Jonah and the stranger made it to the top of the ravine.

The four-wheeler driver nodded to the other man. "I'll take it from here."

"Are you sure?" Jonah asked, frowning. "He's pretty much a deadweight."

Jonah was right. With all the jostling, Abe had completely passed out. Liv studied the stranger. As muscular as he was, he couldn't possibly lift Abe by himself.

"I've got him." The stranger lifted Abe into his arms and slid him onto the backseat of the truck.

Despite her anger at the man's driving skills, Liv recognized sheer, brute strength in the man's arms and broad shoulders. That he could lift a full-size man by himself said a lot about his physical abilities.

But it didn't excuse him from making them crash. She quelled her admiration and focused on getting Abe to a medical facility. If the stranger stuck around after they got Abe situated, Liv would tell him exactly what she thought of him.

Chapter Two

Hawkeye couldn't follow through on his pursuit of the other guy on the ATV. Not after the fleeing man caused the farm-truck driver to crash his vehicle into a tree. He'd had to stop to render assistance and pull the older man out of the cab before the engine caught fire, or he and the woman might have died.

"I'll follow on my four-wheeler," Hawkeye offered.

"No need," the woman said. "We can take it from here."

Hawkeye frowned. Though young and pretty, the auburn-haired Miss Dawson's jaw was set. Her brows drew together over deep-green eyes as she climbed into the back of the cab next to the injured truck driver.

Hawkeye wanted to argue, but he didn't. She

was mad at him for something. Then he realized she'd probably only seen one ATV fly out into the road. Hawkeye had been far enough behind the other guy, he hadn't emerged onto the highway until the truck had already gone off the road.

The Dawson woman wouldn't have seen that there were two ATVs. He smiled and turned away, understanding why she was angry, but not feeling the need to explain himself.

He watched as the truck took off. Then he climbed onto his four-wheeler and followed the group back to Grizzly Pass and the only medical facility in a fifty-mile radius.

The clinic was a block from the Blue Moose Tavern—Hawkeye's temporary boss had set up offices in the apartment above the bar. As Hawkeye passed the Blue Moose, Garner stepped out onto the landing and waved at Hawkeye, a perplexed frown pulling his brows low.

Hawkeye nodded briefly, but didn't slow the ATV. Though it was illegal to drive an off-road vehicle on a public road, he held steady, pulled into the clinic driveway and hopped off.

An ambulance had pulled up in the parking lot and EMTs were off-loading a gurney. A sheriff's vehicle was parked nearby.

Olivia Dawson stood beside the truck, talking to Abe and a sheriff's deputy. One of the EMTs shone a light into her eyes.

She pushed his light away. "I'm fine. It's Abe you need to worry about."

"Ma'am, it looks like you hit your head in the accident. You might have a concussion." He insisted on wiping the dried blood from her forehead and applying a small butterfly bandage. "I suggest you see a doctor before you drive yourself anywhere."

"Really, I'm fine." She pushed past him and gripped Abe's hand.

The deputy flipped open a notepad. "Ma'am, could you describe what happened?"

"A four-wheeler darted out in front of us on the highway. We swerved to miss it and crashed into a tree. You might want to send a fire engine to put out the fire and a tow truck to retrieve the truck."

"Will do, ma'am."

"And stop calling me *ma'am*," she said. "I'm not your mother."

The deputy grinned. "No, ma'am. You're not."

Olivia rolled her eyes and turned back to her foreman.

When the EMTs had the stretcher ready, they

rolled it over next to her. She stepped out of the way and stood to the side as they loaded a now-conscious Abe.

The man was obviously in a lot of pain. His pale face broke out in a sweat as the EMTs lowered him onto the stretcher. Once he was settled, he held out a hand to Olivia.

She took it. "Don't worry about me. I can handle the ranch."

"No, Liv, you can't. Things aren't the same as when you left. You need help."

Liv shook her head. "I can work the animals better than most men."

Abe chuckled and winced. "You're right, but you can't do this alone. Promise me you'll get help." His gaze shifted to where Hawkeye stood a few feet away. "Make her get help."

Liv frowned. "You can't ask a stranger to do that."

Abe nodded. "I just did." He waved Hawkeye forward.

Not wanting to get into the midst of a family argument, Hawkeye eased forward. "Sir?"

"I'm Abe Masterson, and you are?"

"Trace Walsh, but my friends call me Hawkeye."

"Hawkeye, this is Olivia Dawson. Olivia,

Hawkeye." Abe lay back, closing his eyes, the effort having cost him. "There, now you aren't strangers. Please, Hawkeye, make sure Olivia doesn't try to run the Stone Oak Ranch alone. She needs dedicated protection. Something's not right out there."

When Hawkeye hesitated, Abe opened his eyes, his gaze capturing Hawkeye's. "Promise."

To appease the injured man, Hawkeye said, "I promise."

The EMT interrupted. "We really need to get Mr. Masterson to the hospital."

"I'm riding with him," Olivia said.

"No." Abe opened his eyes again. "The horses need to be fed and the cattle need to be checked."

"They can wait. You need someone to go with you as your advocate," she insisted. "You might pass out again."

"I didn't pass out," Abe grumbled. "I just closed my eyes."

"Yeah." Olivia snorted. "That's a bunch of bullsh—"

"Uh-uh," Abe interrupted. "You know how your daddy felt about you cursing."

She glared and crossed her arms over her chest. "I'm not a child."

"No, but you don't have to worry about me. I'm alive and still kicking. I can take care of myself. You can visit me at the hospital, if it makes you feel better. But call first. I have a lady friend in Cody. I'm sure she'll come keep me company and put me up until I can get around on my own."

Liv pulled her lip between her teeth and chewed on it before answering. "Are you sure?"

The pucker of Liv's brow and the worried look in her eyes made Hawkeye want to ease her mind. And pull her into his arms. He suspected she wouldn't appreciate the gesture, no matter how well-intentioned. As far as she was concerned, he was the bad guy in this situation. Hawkeye had yet to set the record straight.

"I'm positive," Abe said. "Now let the EMTs do their job. I'd like to get somewhere with a little pain medication. My leg hurts like hell."

Liv backed up quickly, running into Hawkeye's chest.

He reached out to steady her as the medical technicians rolled Abe's gurney away.

"Do you need a ride back to the ranch, Miss Dawson?" Jonah asked. "I have a few errands to run before I head back your way."

Liv nodded. "How long do you need?"

"No more than thirty minutes. I just need to pick up some feed at the feed store and a few groceries for the missus. You're welcome to wait in the truck."

She looked around as if in a daze. "If it's all the same to you, I'd like to pick up dinner from the tavern. I don't think I'll have time to cook anything."

Jonah nodded. "I'll pick you up at the Blue Moose, then."

Hawkeye bit down on his tongue to keep from offering the woman a ride out to her place. No doubt she'd turn it down, preferring a ride from a friend to one from a stranger she thought had caused the wreck.

After Jonah left in his truck, the only two people left on the street were Hawkeye and Liv.

Liv turned to him and poked a finger at his chest, fire burning in her emerald green eyes. "You!"

He raised his hands in surrender. "Me?"

"Don't lay on the innocent act." Her brows drew into a deep V. "Your reckless driving nearly got Abe killed. Give me one good reason why I shouldn't turn you over to the sheriff." She crossed her arms over her chest.

Hawkeye glanced at the damning ATV. "I didn't drive out in front of your pickup."

"Like hell you didn't." Twin flags of pink flew high on her cheekbones. "You didn't even look left or right before you barreled out onto the highway. What if we had been a van full of children? You could have killed an entire family." She flung her arm out.

"It wasn't me." He shook his head. "I was chasing a guy on another four-wheeler."

"Right. Why should I believe you?" Her finger shot out again and poked him in the chest. "You're a stranger. For that matter, why were you on my property?" She jabbed him again. "You were trespassing. I could have you arrest—"

As a sniper, Hawkeye considered himself a patient man. But the finger in the chest was getting to him, and the woman with the green fire blazing from her eyes was far too pretty for him to slug—not that he would ever hit a woman. But she just wasn't going to listen to him unless he did something drastic.

So he grabbed her finger, yanked her up against his body and clamped an arm around her waist, bringing her body tight against his. Then he slammed his lips down on hers. For the first time in the past five minutes, silence reigned.

With one hand captured in Hawkeye's hand, Liv pressed the other to his chest and gave a pathetic attempt at pushing him away. Hawkeye strengthened his hold.

After a few seconds, she quit pushing against him, her fingers curling into his shirt.

Her lips were soft and full beneath his. Even though he'd stemmed her tirade, Hawkeye was in no hurry to raise his head. Instead, he raised his hand, his fingers sliding up to cup the back of her head.

She gasped, her mouth opening to his.

Taking it as an invitation, Hawkeye swept his tongue past her teeth to claim hers in a long, slow caress.

The tension in her body melted away and she leaned into him, her tongue toying with his, giving as good as he gave.

When he finally broke the kiss, he briefly leaned his cheek against her temple, careful not to disturb the bandage on her forehead, and then he straightened.

Liv touched her fingers to her lips, her eyes glazed. "Why did you do that?"

His lips quirked upward. "I couldn't think of

a better way to make you shut up long enough to listen."

Her glaze cleared and her brows met in the middle the second before her hand snapped out and connected with his face in a hard slap.

She raised her hand again, but he caught it before she could hit him again.

"There was another four-wheeler," he said. "I was chasing him. He was a good fifty yards ahead of me when he reached the road. I would have caught him if I hadn't stopped to render aid." He forced her wrist down to her side. "Now, you can choose to believe me or not. But that's what happened."

Liv rubbed her wrist, her eyes narrowing. "That doesn't explain why you were on my land."

"I started out on government land, up in the hills, when I ran across the other man, planting explosives in a valley. I thought it might be a good idea to ask him why he was doing that."

Liv's breath caught in her throat. "Explosives?"

"Yes."

"Why would someone plant explosives in the hills?" she asked.

"I suspect it has something to do with the oil pipeline cutting through that area."

"But why come through my property?"

"I don't know, but if you have livestock, your fence is down in two places. You should get someone to help you put it back up."

She laughed, the sound seeming to border on hysteria. "That someone was just hauled off in an ambulance."

His brows furrowed. "Don't you have ranch hands?"

Liv's red hair had come loose of its ponytail. She reached up to push it back from her face. "Only during roundup. It was just my father and our foreman managing a herd of about five hundred Brangus cows and twenty horses."

"Then you might want to let your father know about the fences."

Liv couldn't stop the sudden burning in her eyes, nor could she speak past the instant tightening of her vocal cords. She had to swallow twice before she could answer. "That would be hard considering we buried him today."

Hawkeye had been in the process of turning away. He froze, his shoulders stiffening. When he faced her again, he stared at her without any expression on his face.

The big man's lack of emotion and the anger he stirred inside her helped Liv keep it together.

"Who else is with you on your ranch?" Hawkeye asked.

She squared her shoulders. "You're looking at the sum total of ranch hands on the Stone Oak Ranch."

His gaze raked over her from top to toe. "You're serious?"

Lifting her chin, Liv faced him with all the bravado of a prizefighter. "I'm fully capable of mending fences and taking care of livestock. I learned to ride a horse before I learned to walk."

"You're alone." His word wasn't a question. It was more of a statement. "Have you been living in a cocoon, lady? Are you even aware of what's been happening around your little community of Grizzly Pass?"

Raising her chin a little higher, Liv met the man's stare. "I haven't been home in the past nine months. My father didn't let me know about any of this. I just got back into town when I was notified of his passing. Now, if you'll excuse me, I have to meet Jonah at the tavern in a few minutes."

She pushed past him and thought that was the end of it.

A hand reached out and grabbed her arm, yanking her back around.

She raised a brow and stared down at Hawkeye's big fingers. "Let go of me."

"You're not safe out on that ranch by yourself. A man with access to dynamite passed through your place."

She had already come to the same conclusion, but knew she didn't have a choice. The ranch couldn't run itself and she'd be damned if she sold out to that greedy, bottom-dwelling Mr. Rausch. "I'm fine on my own. I learned to handle a gun almost as early as I learned to ride a horse. I'm not afraid of being alone."

"You should be." He sighed and released her arm. "Look, at least come with me to talk to my boss. He'll want to hear what's going on out your way."

"Are you crazy?" She shook her head. "I don't know you from Jack."

He held out his hand again. "At the risk of repeating myself, my name's Trace Walsh, but my friends call me—"

She waved away his hand. "Yeah, yeah. They call you Hawkeye." With a shrug, she stared down Main Street toward the tavern. "Just who is your boss?"

"Kevin Garner, an agent for the Department of Homeland Security."

Her curiosity captured, she returned her attention to Hawkeye. "Is that it? Is that why you were out in the mountains? You work for the DHS?"

Hawkeye shook his head. "Not hardly. I'm an army ranger on loan to the DHS. This is only temporary duty to help Garner and his team. He seems to think there's enough activity going on in this area that he needed a hand."

Liv didn't say anything, just stared at the man with the crisp, black hair and incredibly blue eyes. Perhaps Hawkeye's boss was onto something. Liv had never quite swallowed the idea that her father had fallen off his horse and died instantly. He was a good rider. No, he was the best, and had the rodeo buckles to prove it. The man had ridden broncos when he was younger and still broke wild horses. When he was on a horse, he wasn't just on it—he was a part of it. "I guess it wouldn't hurt to talk to your boss." She raised her finger. "But don't ever try to kiss me again."

Hawkeye raised his hands, a smile tugging

at the corners of his lips. Those lips that had awakened a flood of unwanted desire inside Liv. For a stranger, no less. "Don't worry. I like my women willing."

"And quiet."

"Not necessarily." He winked. "Just quiet when they need to be."

"Whatever." She rolled her eyes. "Just don't kiss me. I can do a lot more than slap."

He rubbed the side of his cheek where the red imprint of her hand had just begun to fade. "I'll remember that. Next time we kiss, you'll have to initiate."

"Good. Because that will never happen." She planted her fists on her hips. "So where is your boss? I'd like to get this meeting over with. I have a ride to catch."

"You're in luck. His office is over the Blue Moose Tavern." He flung his leg over the four-wheeler and jerked his head to the rear. "You're welcome to ride with me."

"No, thanks. I'll walk." Liv stepped onto the sidewalk and hurried toward the tavern.

The four-wheeler engine revved behind her. A moment later, Hawkeye pulled up beside her. "Sure you don't want a ride?"

"I'm sure."

He pressed his thumb to the throttle lever and the ATV sped up the street, disappearing around the back of the tavern.

Alone for the rest of the distance to the tavern, Liv had just enough time to think through all that had happened since she'd arrived home. For a moment her predicament threatened to overwhelm her.

Daddy, why did you have to go and die?

She fought to hold back the tears as she came abreast of the building she'd been aiming for.

Hawkeye rounded the corner and tilted his head. "The staircase to Garner's office is over here."

She followed him up a set of wooden stairs to the landing at the top.

Before Hawkeye could knock, the door flew open and a man probably in his midthirties with brown hair and blue eyes stood in the door frame. "Hawkeye, I'm glad you stopped by. The sheriff isn't keen on the folks around here driving their four-wheelers on the main roads."

Hawkeye turned toward Liv. "Kevin, this is Olivia Dawson. Liv, this is Kevin Garner with the DHS."

Garner held out his hand. "Nice to meet you."

His eyes narrowed slightly and he stared hard at her. "Are you any relation to Everett Dawson?"

She nodded, her chest tight. "That was my father."

Garner squeezed her hand in his. "I was sorry to hear about his passing. Everything I've heard from the locals indicated he was a good man."

"One of the best," she added, choking on her barely contained emotion. "They told me he died in a horseback-riding accident."

"That's what we heard from the sheriff. And you think otherwise?" Garner pulled her across the threshold. "Come in. Tell me what you know."

Liv hesitated only a moment before following the man into the interior of what appeared to be more an operations center than an office. Two other men stood beside a large table with maps spread out across its surface.

"If you knew my father, you'd know his being thrown from a horse was highly unlikely."

Garner nodded. "I'd wondered. I understand his ranch butted up against government property."

Liv nodded. "It does."

"Was he having any problems on the ranch? Any evidence of trespassing?"

"I've been away from home for months. He hadn't told me anything and, with funeral arrangements, I haven't had a chance to ride the perimeter." She nodded toward Hawkeye. "I'm told I have a couple of fences down."

"She does. I went through them chasing a man out of the hills on a four-wheeler."

Garner's eyes widened. "Is that why you rode an off-road vehicle on a state highway?"

Hawkeye dipped his head in a brief nod. "I didn't have much of a choice. My truck's back where I parked it at the gravel road leading up to the national forest. While I was following through on the path that pipeline inspector was traveling before he was shot, I ran across a guy planting explosives at the exact location where Khalig was shot and killed."

"What about explosives?" A tall, red-haired man joined Hawkeye and held out his hand to Liv. "Jon Casper. But you can call me Ghost."

She shook his hand, her fingers nearly crushed in his strong grip.

A broad-shouldered man with brown hair and green eyes nudged Ghost aside and held out his hand. "Max Decker. You can call me Caveman."

Yet another man with a high and tight hair-cut held out his hand. "Rex Trainor. US Marine Corps. Most people call me T-Rex."

Liv laughed. "Do any of you go by your given names?"

As one, everyone but Garner replied, "No."

"Guess that answers my question." She shook T-Rex's hand. "Are you all like Hawkeye—military on loan to the DHS?"

T-Rex, Ghost and Caveman nodded.

Ghost held up his hand. "Navy."

Caveman nodded. "Delta Force."

Liv frowned. "Are things that bad around here?"

The three men shrugged.

"Better than being in the sandbox of the Middle East," Ghost said.

"Some of the natives are friendly," Caveman said. "And some…not so much."

Liv leaned around the three big military men. "Anyone else I should be aware of?"

"Yo!" A thin, younger man sat with his back to the others, his hands on a computer keyboard in the corner of the room. He raised his hand without turning away from the array of monitors he faced.

"That's Hack," Hawkeye said. "He's our tech support guy."

"While you get to know each other, I'll call in the sheriff and the state bomb squad." Garner pulled his cell phone from his pocket.

"I don't think the bomb squad will be necessary," Hawkeye said. "I interrupted him before he could connect the detonator. I didn't see anything but the explosive and the fuse."

Ghost grabbed a jacket. "I'll check it out. At the very least we need to retrieve the explosives to keep him from blowing the pipeline."

Caveman slung his own jacket over his shoulder. "The sooner the better."

"The trailer's back where I parked the truck at the base of the mountain," Hawkeye reminded them. "If you're going, you'll have to risk driving the ATVs on public roads. I didn't run into the county cops. But that doesn't mean you'll be so lucky."

"We'll take that risk," Ghost said. "We can cut through some of the less traveled streets."

"Be careful," Hawkeye warned. "He might have circled back to finish the job."

Once the other two men had left the room, Liv cornered Garner. "What the hell is going on here?"

Garner motioned toward the table with the maps. "You got a few minutes?"

She glanced at her watch. "I have about ten before my ride gets here."

"I can get you where you want to go," Garner offered.

She shook her head. "This is all too much. I don't know you, and I don't know what to think about all of this." She waved at the map with the red stars marking locations like a military operation. "First my father, then my foreman. And now you say there was a man with explosives trying to blow up the pipeline? Has the entire county gone crazy? This is Grizzly Pass, not some war-torn country on the other side of the world."

Garner's lips thinned, his face grim. "I've been monitoring this area for the past three months. A lot of internet activity indicated something big was brewing."

Liv nodded. "You're right. I'd say an attempt to blow up the pipeline is pretty big."

He shook his head. "Even bigger. I think there is the potential for some kind of takeover, but we've only scratched the surface."

"Takeover?" Liv's heart thundered in her chest. "Are you kidding me? This is America. Land of the free, home of democracy. We change things by electing new representatives."

"Some people don't like what we're getting." Kevin touched the map. "We've already had flare-ups."

Liv sank into a chair. "Flare-ups? Incidents? Takeovers?" She pinched the bridge of her nose, feeling a headache forming. "This can't be. Not in Grizzly Pass. What do we have here to take over?"

"This is the perfect location to build the equivalent of a small army. There's lots of space to hide nefarious activities. Mountains with caves to store a weapons buildup. People who know how to use guns can train in the backwoods where no one knows what they are doing."

"Sweet heaven, and I thought the worst thing about coming home was burying my father," Liv said. "I can't take in any more of this. I have to go through my father's effects, make arrangements with the lawyer and the bank, not to mention the animals to tend and a fence to mend."

Garner's gaze shot to Hawkeye. "Accidental or cut?"

"From what I could tell, cut," Hawkeye answered for her. "My bet is that the man setting the charges cut the fence to give him access to government land without going the usual route."

"How many acres is the Stone Oak Ranch?" Garner asked.

"Over five thousand."

He stared down at the contour map. "Lots of hills and valleys."

"There are. We're in the foothills of the Beartooth Mountains," Liv said.

Garner glanced up at Hawkeye. "It bears watching."

Liv's belly knotted. She wasn't at all sure she liked the intent look on the DHS man's face. "What do you mean?"

"Your ranch is in a prime location for trouble. Who do you have working there? Do they know how to use a gun? Do you trust them?" Garner asked.

Hawkeye snorted. "You're looking at 'them.' Miss Dawson is the only person left to run the ranch."

"I don't need anyone's help. If I need additional assistance, I'll hire someone." Liv stood. "All this conspiracy-theory talk is just that—

talk. I have work to do. If you'll excuse me, I have a ride to catch."

Garner stepped in front of her. "You don't understand. You could be in grave danger."

"I can handle it." She tilted her head. "I really need to go." She stepped around the man and ran into Hawkeye.

"Garner's right. You can't run a ranch and watch your back at the same time."

"Let me assign one of my men to the ranch. Then you'll get some help and we can take our time making certain the group responsible for the recent troubles isn't conducting their business on your property or the neighboring federal land."

Liv shook her head. "I can hire my own help."

"The men on my team are trained combatants. We think the group planning the takeover are training like soldiers. One of their men had a shooting range and training facility on his ranch."

Liv tilted her head and stared at Garner through narrowed eyes. "Sounds to me like you already know who is involved in this coup or whatever it is."

"We've only just begun to scratch the surface. Someone is supplying weapons on a large scale." Garner took her hand. "Someone with money."

Liv's blood chilled. "You're not kidding, are you?"

Garner's lips firmed. "I wish I was."

She pulled her hand from his and pushed her hair back from her face, wishing she had a rubber band to secure it. "Why do you need my ranch?"

"Stone Oak Ranch is right in the middle of everything." Garner pointed to the map. "You said yourself you didn't think your father could have fallen off his horse. He was too good of a rider. What if he didn't fall off his horse?"

Her gut clenched and she tightened her fingers into fists. "What do you mean? Do you think someone killed him?" Dear Lord, what had happened to her father?

Garner lifted his shoulders slightly. "We don't know, but if someone was out there, your father could have run across something that person didn't want to get out."

A sick, sinking feeling settled in the pit of Liv's belly. "When my father's horse returned without his rider, my foreman went looking for him. He found my father on the far northwest corner of the ranch, where he'd gone to check the fences." Liv swallowed hard on the lump rising in her throat. "That corner of the property borders federal land."

"Olivia, let me position one of my men on your property," Garner pleaded. "He can appear to hire on as a ranch hand and help you mend the fences. It will give him the opportunity to keep an eye out for trouble, while protecting you."

Liv bristled. "I don't need someone to protect me."

"No one can watch his or her own back," Hawkeye said. "As a member of the armed forces, I know what it means to trust the guys behind me. You need a battle buddy."

"I do want to find out if my father was murdered. And who might have done it." Liv chewed on her lip a moment before sighing. "Who did you have in mind?"

Garner smiled. "The only other man still in this room besides me."

A thrill of something she hadn't felt in a long time—if you didn't count the recent kiss—rippled through Liv. Taking on Hawkeye could prove to be a big mistake in more ways than one. "What choice do I have?"

"None," Hawkeye said, his tone firm and final.

For however long it took to find her father's murderer and stop this insanity going on in her community, she was stuck with Hawkeye. And despite her initial reticence, she had to admit to herself she might just need him.

"Don't look so worried. You can trust Hawkeye," Garner said with a smile and a wave before he turned to go back to the maps spread across the table.

It wasn't Hawkeye she didn't trust. What bothered her most was the reaction she'd had to his kiss. Hell, she wasn't sure she could trust herself around the rugged army ranger.

Chapter Three

"We'll get that meal you wanted and then we'll head for your place." Hawkeye cupped Liv's elbow and guided her through the loft apartment's door.

For once she didn't argue or pull away.

Hawkeye counted that as progress.

"Damn. The sun's already setting." Olivia shaded her eyes and looked toward the west.

"We can skip the tavern and head right for the ranch," Hawkeye offered.

She shook her head. "You said yourself that your truck is where you left it on a dirt road. By the time we retrieve it and make it back to the ranch, it'll already be dark. We might as well get something to eat and take it with us. I can guarantee there's nothing edible that doesn't have to be cooked at the ranch." She started down the steps ahead of him.

"I'll be down in ten minutes to take you out to Hawkeye's truck." Garner followed them onto the landing. "You'll need it with Liv's farm truck out of commission."

"The sheriff called a tow truck," Olivia said. "The way it was smoking, I'm sure my dad's old truck is a total loss." Her lips turned downward. "I'll be in the market for a used, *cheap* truck or we won't be able to haul the hay to the barn before winter."

"You can use mine until then," Hawkeye offered.

Instead of nodding, she frowned. "I can't rely on a man who is at best a temporary solution to a much larger problem."

"That being?" Hawkeye asked.

"I need more than a truck out at the ranch. I need my foreman, or at least someone who can do some of the heavy work. Tossing hay bales isn't easy." She chewed on her bottom lip.

The motion made Hawkeye's groin tighten. He wanted to pull that lip into his mouth and kiss her worries away.

Why?

He didn't know. He'd just met the woman.

That she was willing to risk her life to pull a full-grown man out of a smoking truck said a lot about her character. Not only was she strong, she was tough and cared about the people around her.

"I'll be at the ranch," Hawkeye said. "While I'm keeping an eye on things, I can help with hay hauling and doing other chores as needed."

Olivia snorted. "Thanks, but you won't be around for long. I'm sure, once Kevin and his team figure out what's going on, you'll be back with your unit. I need a permanent solution. It took both my father and our foreman to manage the ranch with seasonal help. Even if Abe wasn't laid up with a broken leg, I'd have to find more help. The kind that will stick around for the long haul."

Hawkeye raised his hands palms up and smiled. "In the meantime, you have me. Use me while you're advertising for additional staff. What can it hurt? You're getting my services free."

Olivia's stiff shoulders relaxed slightly. "You're right. And thanks."

"Don't sound so ungrateful. Wait until you see what I can do. I'm strong, and I've hauled my share of hay in my younger days." He stopped at the bottom of the staircase and pulled Olivia around to face him. "And I have a special skill." His lips twitched.

Her breath hitched and her gaze dropped to his lips. "Oh yeah?" she said, her voice a whisper.

Hawkeye leaned toward her, as if he might kiss her, his lips passing her mouth and going toward her ear. "I know the difference between a steer and a cow." He leaned back and smiled. Yes, he was flirting with her, but he could tell she needed a little levity in a bad situation. Having lost her father and now with her foreman off the ranch, she had a lot weighing on her shoulders. Hawkeye winked.

Olivia's lips pressed into a tight line.

Not exactly the reaction he was aiming for. For a moment, Hawkeye thought he might have gone too far flirting with the pretty rancher, and she might slap his face again. Just in case, he leaned back a little farther.

A moment passed and Olivia's firm lips loosened and spread into a wry smile. "You don't know how important a skill that is." She stuck out her hand. "For however long you're here, you're hired."

With an accord reached, Hawkeye shook her

hand, an electric shock running up his arm and shooting low into his groin. The woman had an effect on him he hadn't counted on. Rather than kissing her, like he wanted to, he turned her toward the tavern entrance and ushered her inside with a hand at the small of her back. With everything going wrong in Grizzly Pass, helping Olivia was the first thing that felt right.

As Hawkeye opened the door, a young man was thrown through. He stumbled, fell and landed on his knees on the sidewalk.

A man with a scruffy beard and unkempt brown hair lurched through the door, his face red and splotchy, his breath reeking of booze. "No damned stepson of mine is going to be a dishwasher in a saloon, carrying out other people's trash." He pointed a finger at the boy. "Get home, where you belong. You have your own chores to do."

Olivia crouched to help the teen to his feet.

Once upright, the young man shrugged off her hands and faced the angry man. "I finished the chores before I came to town."

"Don't talk back to me, boy," the man growled.

Hawkeye recognized the drunk man as one of the men Garner had on his watch list. Ernie

Martin. A man who had a gripe with the government over the discontinuance of the subsidies on his livestock.

"Get back to the ranch," Ernie said.

The teen lifted his chin and set his feet slightly apart as if ready to do battle. "I have a job. I need to be here when I said I would."

"Did your mother tell you that you should get a job?" Ernie snorted. "Is she too lazy to get out and get one for herself and bring a little income home for once?"

The teen's fists clenched. "My mother isn't lazy. She has three small children to raise. She'd never make enough money to pay for child care."

"And whose fault is that? She shouldn't have had all those brats."

The teen's eyes narrowed. "You should have stayed off of her. They're your kids, too. And what are you doing to put food on the table? My mother should never have married you."

"She's lucky to be off the reservation. And you should be thankful I took you in out of the goodness of my own heart."

With a snort, the teen brushed the dust off his jeans. "You didn't do either of us any favors."

Ernie's face flushed even redder. "Why, you

ungrateful little brat. That's all the bull crap I'm taking from you." He launched himself at the teen.

Before he'd gone two steps, Hawkeye grabbed Ernie's arm and jerked him around. "Leave the kid alone."

Ernie glared at Hawkeye through glazed eyes, cocked his fist and swung.

Hawkeye caught the fist in his own palm and forced the man's hand down to his side. "Take another swing and I won't go as easy on you." He fished the man's keys out of his pocket and then shoved the man backward, out of range of landing another punch. "You'll have to find a ride home."

Sheriff Scott pulled up in his county sheriff's SUV, parked and got out. "What's going on here?"

Ernie stalked up to the sheriff. "This man stole my keys and threatened me with bodily harm." He pointed at Hawkeye. "Arrest him." The stern tone was offset when the man belched, sending out a vile fog of booze-heavy breath.

"Now, Ernie, I'm sure there's another side to this story," the sheriff said.

"It's cut-and-dried." Ernie pointed at the keys in Hawkeye's hands. "He has my keys."

Sheriff Scott leaned away from Ernie's face. "The man's doing you a favor and keeping you from getting a DUI." He stared at Ernie. "How much have you had to drink?"

"Just one beer," Ernie said. "A man's got a right to drink a beer. Or is our government going to take that right away, too?"

The sheriff crossed his arms over his chest. "Care to take a Breathalyzer test?"

Ernie opened his mouth and had just enough sense left to close it again before his alcohol-soaked brain let his mouth loose.

Hawkeye almost laughed, but knew it would only rile the man more.

"Hop in, Ernie. I'll give you a ride home."

The man folded his arms over his chest and dug his heels into the concrete sidewalk. "Ain't leaving my truck here."

"I'll drive it home," the teen offered.

Ernie shot a narrow-eyed glare at the young man. "You ain't touching my damned truck."

The teen raised his hands. "Okay. I won't drive your truck."

"Don't worry about it, CJ," the sheriff assured him. He turned to Ernie. "I'll have my deputies bring your truck out to your house in the morning, after you've had a chance to sober up. You shouldn't be driving anymore tonight." Sheriff Scott hooked Ernie's elbow and eased him toward the backseat.

Ernie jerked loose of the sheriff's hold and pointed a finger at the teen. "You're done with this job. I didn't approve of it anyway."

The teen stood with his feet braced apart, his jaw set. "I'm going to work."

"Not as a dishwasher, you aren't. I won't have members of this community pointing at you, feeling sorry for poor Ernie Martin's stepson who has to work to support his family."

"I don't care what you call it—I want my sisters and brother to have something to eat. It's either here or somewhere else."

"I provide," Ernie insisted. "And it ain't your place to be telling tales about what goes on at home."

CJ's fists clenched. "I'm going to have a job."

"Not here, you're not," Ernie said with a finality that made CJ blink.

"How about at my place?" Olivia stepped forward. "Mr. Martin, you might not remember me, but I'm Olivia Dawson, Everett Dawson's daughter."

"Yeah. So?" He ignored her outstretched hand. "That doesn't give you the right to butt into a private conversation."

Hawkeye had to stop himself from snorting. The way Ernie had been yelling, the entire town of Grizzly Pass had to have heard his "private" conversation.

Olivia continued. "Since my father passed—" she swallowed hard and pressed on "—my foreman has broken his leg. I could use some help. CJ can work for me out at the ranch. He can make some money to tide you over to better times, or at least pay for his own meals." Olivia caught Ernie's stare and held it. "What do you say? You and my father were friends at one time. He'd be proud to have your stepson help me out."

Ernie bristled. "If you need help, why not me?"

Olivia smiled gently.

Hawkeye could feel himself melt. The woman needed to smile more often. She went from pretty to stunning in less than a second.

"I wouldn't dream of taking you away from your ranch. I know how hard it is to keep things running. Besides, I can't afford to pay much."

"I'll take it," CJ said. He turned to his stepfather. "I'll do my chores before I leave the house and when I get back."

"And how will you get there and back?" Ernie asked, a sneer pulling at one side of his mouth. "You have school starting in a couple weeks."

"I'll manage."

Ernie snorted and turned back to Olivia. "If he steals something, don't come crying to me. He's been nothing but a pain in my rear since I brought him to the ranch."

CJ's eyes flashed, but he kept his mouth firmly shut. How he put up with Ernie, Hawkeye had no idea. Just standing near the belligerent jerk made Hawkeye itch to shove his fist in the man's face.

"Fine." Ernie waved at Olivia and his stepson. The drunk swayed and practically fell into the backseat of the sheriff's SUV. As he leaned out to close the door, he said, "He's your problem now."

"You got a way home, CJ?" Sheriff Scott asked.

The teen nodded. "Yes, sir." He glanced toward the sheriff's vehicle as if it was the last place he wanted to be.

The sheriff shook his head and slid behind

the wheel. A moment later, all Hawkeye could see of Ernie Martin were the taillights of the sheriff's SUV disappearing at the end of Main Street.

Olivia clapped her hands together. "Well, that was lovely. I have the help I needed." She smiled at CJ. "How soon can you start?"

The young man dug his hands into his pockets. "If it's all the same to you, I'd like to start in the morning. Right now, I need to get home." He gazed in the direction his stepfather had gone.

"Do you need a ride?" Hawkeye asked.

CJ shook his head. "No, sir. I'll just let my boss know I can't work here anymore. I have a bicycle. I'll get myself home."

"That's got to be about five miles out of town. And it's getting dark." Olivia frowned. "Let one of us take you."

The young man shook his head. "I'll need my bike to get to work in the morning."

"I live three miles out of town," Olivia said. "Between you living on one side of Grizzly Pass and me on the other, that's over eight miles several times a day. You need some other way to get there and back."

"I promise." CJ stepped forward. "I can do

it. I'm used to riding long distances. It's nothing." He edged toward the tavern. "I really need to get home."

Olivia still frowned, but she stepped out of the youth's way. "Tell you what—don't worry. We'll figure something out."

"Thank you, Miss Dawson. I'll be there in the morning, right after I do my chores." The teen darted into the tavern, leaving Hawkeye and Liv where they'd been when the ruckus started.

"Are you two ready to go?" a voice said behind Hawkeye. Kevin Garner descended to the bottom step of the staircase leading up to the loft apartment.

"Not quite. We had a little delay." Olivia started to reach for the door.

Hawkeye beat her to it and opened it wide for her and Garner. As his boss passed, Hawkeye nodded. "I'll fill you in as we wait for our orders."

Chapter Four

Liv cradled the food containers on her lap in the backseat of Kevin Garner's truck.

The Homeland Security agent dropped them off at Hawkeye's truck where he'd left it parked with the utility trailer. After disconnecting the trailer from his truck, Hawkeye rolled it around to the back of Garner's and dropped it onto the hitch.

Garner helped Liv into Hawkeye's truck and then extended a hand. "Be careful and let me know of anything out of the ordinary, even if it seems inconsequential. All the little pieces add up."

Liv fumbled with the food, but managed to take the man's hand. "I haven't been home in nine months. How am I supposed to know what is out of the ordinary?"

"Anything strange and unusual, just give me a buzz." He squeezed her hand.

Liv snorted. "Things seem to have changed drastically. This used to be a nice, quiet community filled with neighbors who looked out for each other."

"Apparently, trouble has been brewing for years," Garner said. "Antigovernment sentiment isn't new."

"I suppose." Liv sighed. "I loved being on the ranch and working hard. I guess I didn't have time to hang out on the street corners grousing about what I couldn't change."

With one last squeeze, Garner released Liv's hand. "Trust Hawkeye and your own instincts."

Hawkeye slid into the driver's seat and started the engine. "Ready?"

Using the food containers as an excuse not to look Hawkeye in the face, she nodded. "Ready as I'll ever be." For a moment, the events of the past few days threatened to consume her. This was not the homecoming she'd anticipated at the end of her five-year promise.

All through college and the three years following graduation, Liv could think of nothing she wanted more than to come home to Grizzly Pass. Her promise to her father had kept her in

Seattle. Now she was back in the county and the thought of going to the home she grew up in nearly tore her apart.

She sat in the passenger seat, a lump the size of her fist blocking her throat, her eyes burning from unshed tears.

"I take it we go out the way we came into town?" Hawkeye cast a glance in her direction.

All Liv could do was nod, afraid if she tried to get a word past her vocal cords, she'd break down and cry. And what good would crying do now? It wouldn't bring her father back. Crying wouldn't unbreak Abe's leg and make everything all right again. Nothing could fix her world. All she could do was to take one day, one hour and one breath at a time. Her father had taught her a long time ago that cowgirls didn't cry.

Damn you, Dad. This one does.

As they neared the gated entrance to Stone Oak Ranch, her chest tightened and she couldn't manage to take that one breath.

When Hawkeye didn't slow, Liv was forced to squeak out, "Turn here!"

Hawkeye jammed his foot on the brake pedal. The truck skidded to a stop in the middle of the highway, several yards past the ranch entrance.

Liv flew forward. The seat belt across her torso snapped tight, keeping her from jettisoning through the windshield.

"You could give me a little more warning next time." Hawkeye shifted into Reverse and backed up several yards. Then he drove up to the gate.

Liv shot out a hand, touching his shoulder.

Again, he hit the brakes and turned to her. "What?"

The relentless pressure on her chest refused to subside. "I can't breathe," she whispered. "I can't breathe."

"What's wrong?" Hawkeye's brows dived toward the bridge of his nose. "Olivia, look at me. Tell me what's wrong." He reached for her.

She shrank from his hands. If he touched her, she'd fall apart. And she couldn't fall apart. Not now. With her father and her foreman gone, she was all that was left of what had once been her small family. Who else would take care of the animals, the fences, the house and the ranch?

No matter how hard she tried, Liv couldn't seem to get enough air into her starving lungs. She punched the buckle on her seat belt, shoved open her door and dropped down out of the truck. Her legs refused to hold her and she fell to her knees. A sob rose up past the knot in her throat, coming out as a keening wail. Liv clamped a hand over her mouth, praying Hawkeye hadn't heard.

The sound of a truck door opening and closing spurred her to her feet. She didn't want anyone to see her as her composure shattered and she fell apart. Especially not the stranger she'd just met. Hugging her grief to her chest, she ran.

A tear slipped from the corner of her eye, then another and another, until she couldn't do anything to stem the flow. Soon, she couldn't see the road in front of her.

The footsteps pounding behind her made her run faster. "Leave me alone," she cried out. "Just leave me alone."

Hands descended on her shoulders.

Liv jerked free, tripped, regained her footing and took off. Where, she didn't know.

Then something big and heavy hit her from behind, sending her flying forward. She hit the ground hard enough to knock the breath out of her lungs. A heavy mass landed on top of her, pressing her into the dirt and leaves.

She lay still, tears falling and silent sobs racking her body.

The weight on top of her shifted and rolled to the side. Big hands lifted her off the ground and pulled her into a lap and up against a solid wall of muscles.

"Shh, darlin'. Everything's going to be all right." Hawkeye's deep voice rumbled in his chest where Liv pressed her ear.

"H-how can everything be all right?" She hiccuped and more sobs racked her body. "My father is d-dead. I'm going home to a house where he sh-should be, but isn't. Even Abe is g-gone."

"Abe will be back sooner than you think." Hawkeye held her cradled in his lap, smoothing the hair from her damp cheeks. "I'm sorry about your father. He must have been a good man to have you as his daughter."

"The best." She turned her face into Hawkeye's shirt and leaned her cheek against his chest, breathing in the outdoorsy scent she would forever associate with this man. The tears slowed to a trickle and her breathing began to return to normal. "He would have liked you, I think."

Hawkeye chuckled. "You think? You mean you don't know?"

"He had a great respect for the men and women who served in the armed forces."

For a long moment, Liv sat in Hawkeye's lap, absorbing some of his strength to tide her over when she entered the house she had grown up in, empty now of both of her parents.

Finally, she squared her shoulders and leaned away from Hawkeye. Wiping the remaining tears from her cheeks, she gave him a weak smile. "I'm sorry. I don't normally fall apart like that."

"You're allowed." Hawkeye tucked a strand of her hair behind her ear. "You haven't had the best of days." He bent and touched his lips to her forehead, avoiding the bandaged area.

God, it felt good. A kiss on her mouth would be even better. A flood of desire washed over her with an awareness of where she was. Seated across Hawkeye's lap, she could feel the hard evidence of his own reaction to her pressing against her bottom.

She swayed toward him, her lips tingling in anticipation of touching his. Everything would be better, all of her pain would be eased, if she just kissed him.

Hawkeye's arms tightened around her, bringing her closer.

When her lips were a mere breath from his, a sound penetrated the deepening dusk. The urgent, distressed bawling of cattle.

"Shh." Liv stiffened, her pulse quickening. "Do you hear that?"

"Yeah." Hawkeye's hands gripped Liv around the waist. He lifted her out of his lap, scrambled to stand and pulled her up beside him.

"Come on." Liv grabbed his hand and ran for the truck.

Hawkeye jumped into the driver's seat.

Liv climbed in on the passenger side and rolled down her window, trying to hear over the rumble of the engine. Again, the sound of cattle mooing reached her. Something was wrong. At dusk cattle settled in for the night, quietly chewing their cud. Wishing she could put her own foot on the accelerator, Liv clenched her fists and willed Hawkeye to go faster.

The driveway up to the ranch house and barn curved through a stand of trees. Finally, it opened to a rounded knoll, on top of which stood her family home, a two-story colonial with a wide, sweeping wraparound porch.

Liv pushed aside the stabbing sadness, her thoughts on the cattle and horses for which she was now responsible. "Head for the barn at the back of the house," she instructed.

Hawkeye drove around to the barn and shone his headlights at the corral and pasture beyond.

Cattle moved about in a frenzied stirring of dust. A horse whinnied, the muffled sound carrying through the wooden panels of the barn. The sharp crack of hooves kicking at the insides of a stall made Liv jump.

"What the hell's going on?" She jumped down from the truck and ran for the barn.

"Olivia!" Hawkeye shouted behind her.

She didn't wait for him to catch up to her. There was a rifle locked in the tack room inside the barn. If a pack of wolves was stalking the livestock, it wouldn't be long before the wolves cornered one and took it down. Or worse, the entire herd, situated near the barn, could stampede and trample over each other.

Ripping her keys out of her pocket, Liv entered the barn, slapped the switch on the wall… and nothing. No light came on. She felt her way in the dark to the tack-room door, fumbled for a few seconds trying to find the right key and then jammed it into the lock.

Pushing through, she raced for the desk she could see with the limited light from the western horizon shining through the dingy window. She found the box of bullets her father and Abe kept handy. They never knew when they'd need to shoot a rattlesnake or scare off a wolf or bear. Her father had shown her the stash of bullets and the gun a number of times, stressing that waving her arms wouldn't necessarily frighten wolves or bears. She needed a little more assurance the more dangerous predators wouldn't decide to go for her instead of a tasty cow or horse.

Liv tipped the box over, poured bullets on the desk, grabbed a few and stuffed some into her jeans pocket. Then she stretched her arms upward, going for the rifle hanging on hooks over the door. She wasn't quite tall enough to reach it. She jumped, trying to push it off the hooks.

"Need a hand?" Hawkeye appeared in the doorway and, with very little effort, lifted the rifle off the wall and handed it to her.

"Something's out there," she said, though she knew she was stating the obvious.

"I have a gun. Do you want me to fire off a round?" He held up a nine-millimeter handgun she could just make out in the dim light from the window.

"Not yet." She grabbed the spotlight they

kept plugged into a wall socket and shoved it toward the man. "See if that works while I load this rifle."

Hawkeye clicked a button and the room lit up.

With the light on, Liv was able to load the rifle quickly. As soon as she shot the bolt home, she slipped past Hawkeye and into the barn.

A horse whinnied and kicked the side of his stall.

"Shh, Stormy. I'll be back in a minute," Liv said and stepped outside into the barnyard.

The livestock continued to move, churning up a cloud of dust.

Liv coughed and pulled her shirt up over her mouth and nose. "I can't see a damned thing. I'll have to go out there."

"No way," Hawkeye responded. "You'll be trampled."

"I have to get upwind of them to see what's causing them to be so nervous. If you don't want to risk it, stay here." She didn't wait for his response. Instead, she ran along the split-rail fence away from the bulk of the herd. Soon the dust thinned and the first stars of the night twinkled above.

Liv climbed to the top of the rail, swung her

leg over and would have dropped down, but for the hand holding her back.

"Let go," she said. "There might be a bear or a pack of wolves out there."

"Exactly." He shook his head, shining his light toward the cloud of dust that was the herd. "You can't handle it on your own."

"The hell I can't." Liv held up her rifle.

"Trust me, wolves will see you before you see them. If it's a bear, one or two bullets might not be enough to stop him and he won't give you time to reload."

"I can't stay here and do nothing. So either you come with me or let go of my arm so I can do this alone."

Hawkeye hesitated a moment and then let go of her arm.

Liv swallowed her disappointment. She couldn't expect him to step into harm's way over a bunch of cattle that didn't belong to him. She dropped to the ground and started toward the herd.

The spotlight bounced several times across the herd and jerked toward the heavens. The sound of something landing on the ground behind her made her turn.

Hawkeye hurried toward her. "Anyone ever

tell you that you're stubborn?" He moved past her, wielding the flashlight in one hand and his pistol in the other.

"More times than I can count." The corners of Liv's lips quirked upward and she followed this stranger who'd volunteered to walk into a potential stampede. Perhaps he wasn't a lost cause after all. "Anyone ever tell you a nine-millimeter bullet won't down a bear unless you're within kissing distance?"

HAWKEYE'S HEART SKIPPED a few beats and then hammered on. "I'll save my kisses for pretty ranchers with a lot of chutzpah and attitude. Now shut up and look for what's bothering your livestock." Based on her earlier reaction to his kiss and him holding her in his arms, he'd bet his favorite weapon Liv was feeling some of the same attraction he was.

As he hurried toward the herd of cattle, shining the spotlight around the periphery of the clump of dust and the bovines, he couldn't help but wonder if getting involved with Liv would be a big mistake.

Sure, she was pretty, strong and interesting. And, yeah, she fit in his arms like no other woman he'd held in his past. But what happened when the Grizzly Pass troubles were over? He'd be back with his unit several states away. She'd be on this ranch, fighting against wolves and bears alone.

His chest tightened. The thought of one lone woman defending her livelihood with no backup bothered him. The teenager would assist, but he'd be back in school as soon as summer was over. Who would help her then? And how much could a teen do when things got really bad? Predatory animals usually attacked at night. CJ would be back at his home. Olivia would be alone again.

Her best bet would be to hire more help or sell the ranch. One person, man or woman, couldn't single-handedly run a place the size of Stone Oak Ranch.

It had been years since Hawkeye had lived on a ranch. He'd grown up as the foreman's son, not the owner. He'd learned how to rope, brand, vaccinate, castrate and tag steers almost before he could ride a bicycle. He'd planned to spend his life working on a ranch.

All that had changed when he was sixteen. That summer he'd lost his love for ranching when his little sister had died. So many things changed with Sarah's passing.

Yet here he was on a ranch, standing in a field full of restless cows in the murky darkness.

He hefted the flashlight in his hand and panned the pasture, searching for whatever had spooked the livestock.

A shadowy movement caught his attention and made his pulse leap. When he swung the light back toward it, cattle leaped and darted back the opposite direction. If something was there, it couldn't be seen through the milling jumble of crazed animals.

What had him more concerned was that the cattle had completely changed direction and were now headed straight for him and Olivia.

"Get back to the fence!" he shouted.

"Not until we find out what's spooking them," Olivia argued.

"They're coming this way. Run!" Hawkeye aimed his pistol into the air and fired off a round.

The herd didn't veer off course. They charged forward, increasing their speed.

Short of shooting every last one of them, Hawkeye wasn't going to stop the beasts' forward momentum. No amount of waving his arms and shouting would detour them to another direction.

Knowing they had only seconds to spare, Hawkeye spun and ran toward Olivia. "Go! Go! Go!" With his arm holding the flashlight, he circled her back and propelled her toward the fence.

Olivia ran several steps, tripped and fell to her knees.

Flinging the spotlight as far from himself as possible, Hawkeye scooped his arms beneath Olivia's legs, flung her over his shoulder, firefighter style, and sprinted for the nearest split-rail fence.

When he reached it, he dropped Olivia onto her feet on the other side and leaped up onto the rail as the stampede bore down on him. He was able to pull his legs over the top, just in time to avoid being speared by a wayward horn, flung to the ground and trampled to death.

Hawkeye lowered himself to the ground beside Olivia and bent over, sucking in huge, gulping breaths.

Olivia ran to the fence and watched as the cattle raced by, bumping into the rails in their desperate attempt to get away from whatever had frightened them. She coughed and rubbed her eyes, shaking her head. "I can't see anything."

Dust swirled around them so thickly, they could barely see each other, much less the cattle, but they could hear them as they moved past.

When the thunder of hooves faded into the far corner of the pasture, Olivia climbed the fence again.

"Where do you think you're going?" Hawk-eye asked.

"I have to see what was after them."

He caught her around the waist and pulled her down in front of him, his hands resting on her hips. "You can't until the dust settles."

"But someone has to."

He waved his hand out to the side. "You can barely see your hand in front of your face. As soon as you get out into that dust, you won't be able to tell left from right and you won't be able to find your way back to the fence or the barn."

"It won't be dusty forever."

"Exactly. We'll wait until it settles."

"But—"

"If you got out there in that fog of dirt, and the herd came back in your direction, you wouldn't know which way to run. You'll have lost sight of the fence and be unable to get out of their way this time." He shook his head. "I can't let you go."

Her eyes narrowed. "You can't keep me here."

He released her. "You're right. I can't keep you here. But if you go out there, not only are you risking your life, you're risking mine, as well."

She placed her foot on the bottom rail of the fence. "Not if you don't come with me."

"If you go, I'll go. If we both die, my death will be on your hands."

She lowered her foot and stared up at him. "I'd be dead, so I wouldn't know any better."

"What if I died trying to rescue you, and by some miracle you survived?"

She chewed on that confounded lip again, making Hawkeye want to suck it into his mouth and kiss her. Even though she was covered from head to toe in a fine layer of dust, and looked like a dark specter in the night, she still had a way of making him want to shake her and kiss her all at once.

He reached for her hand. "Come on, admit it. You'd feel bad, if this adorable face was crushed in a stampede." He smiled, figuring if he was as dirty as she was, all she'd see was the white of his teeth shining in the darkness.

"Maybe."

"You'd miss your chance to kiss me again."

She glanced away. "I didn't say I *wanted* to kiss you again."

"Sweetheart, you didn't have to say it." With a finger pressed to her chin, he turned her to face him.

As the dust slowly drifted toward the earth, the moon climbed into the sky, transforming the remaining particles of dirt into sparkling diamond dust swirling around her in the darkness.

Olivia opened her mouth—probably to tell him he was wrong, he assumed. Instead she asked, "Big claim for a man who's covered in dirt." Her words came out in a breathy kind of whisper, as if she didn't have quite enough air in her lungs.

"Darlin', you're covered in the same blanket of dust and it doesn't make me want to kiss you any less."

She lifted her chin. "You're insane."

"You're beautiful." He pulled her close and settled his hands on her hips.

"You realize this will never work." Olivia rested her palms on his chest.

"Honey, how difficult can this be? All it takes is two sets of lips with two willing individuals."

"I'm not willing," she insisted.

"Oh no?" He bent to her, his mouth hovering over hers. "Tell me you're not willing again, and I'll forget this kiss."

She stood still, her body tense. What little resistance she'd first exerted changed as her fingers curled into his shirt.

For a moment, Hawkeye thought she might tell him she wasn't willing again and he'd have to end the night frustrated and even more determined to win a kiss from her full, luscious, albeit dusty, lips.

"Afraid?" he whispered, his mouth so close to hers he could feel the warmth of her breath.

Then she tipped upward on her toes and closed the distance in a brief meeting of mouths.

She might have moved away, if Hawkeye had let her, but his hands clasped her hips tightly and he dragged her body against his. He slid his fingers up her back, threading them into her thick auburn hair, disturbing the fine layer of dust. "You call that a kiss?"

She leaned her head back and stared up into his eyes. "I call it insanity."

"Let me show you how it's done." He claimed her mouth in a long, sensuous kiss that sucked the air from his lungs and the starch from his knees.

She opened to him, her lips parting on a gasp.

Before she could change her mind and withdraw from the kiss, he swept in and tasted her tongue, caressing it with his own in a long, sensuous glide.

She might have resisted at first, but her tongue met his in her own dance, tangling and teasing until they finally broke apart, breathless, the cool night air doing nothing to chill the heat building between them.

A distant howl pierced the night sky, answered by the restless moos of the herd on the far side of the pasture.

"I guess I'd better find my rifle and bed down under the stars."

"You're kidding, right?" He thumbed a path through the dust on her cheek. "You can't sleep out here."

"I can and will." Olivia chuckled, the sound tugging at Hawkeye's insides. "What? Are you afraid of the dark?"

"Not hardly. Just what's in it."

"I'm not leaving the livestock to fend for themselves. If that howl was any indication, wolves were behind this little midnight raid. I'm not letting them steal even one calf."

Hawkeye kissed her briefly and turned her toward the house. "Then you'd better get your shower first. I have a sleeping bag in my truck that will fit both of us, but I'd rather not fill it with dust."

"Not to worry." Olivia stepped back and brushed at the dust on her jeans. "I have my own bag."

"It gets downright cold here at night." He tilted his head. Yeah, he'd just met her. Yeah, he was pushing the envelope, but hopefully his flirting would help her forget about the bad stuff. If only for a few minutes. "Sure you don't want to share mine?"

"Not a chance."

"Then go make some mud in the shower. I'll keep an eye on things out here."

She pointed to the barn. "There's a shower in the barn, if you want to get one, too."

"I'll do that. Now go, before I'm tempted to kiss you again."

Chapter Five

Olivia turned and ran toward the house, her footsteps slowing as she neared the structure. Memories crowded in on her as she stepped up onto the porch. Her mother and father had sat with her in that swing when she was a little girl. It had taken her years before she'd sat in it again without wanting to cry over the loss of her mother to cancer.

Not until she stood at the back door did she realize she'd left the keys in the door lock of the tack room. Then she remembered the spare key. Liv lifted the flower on the porch and retrieved the key taped to the bottom where her father had always left it. Some things never changed.

And some things changed forever.

She slipped the key in the lock and turned the knob at the same time. The door swung open, and the scent of home wrapped around her, threatening to drag her to her knees. She didn't have time to wallow in grief. Hawkeye waited outside for her return.

Squaring her shoulders, she entered the kitchen and hurried through the house to her bedroom. Once there, she rifled through her drawers, pulling out fresh underwear, jeans and a sweatshirt. The nights got cold in the high country, even in the summer. Armed with her clothes, careful not to let them brush against her dust-covered body, she crossed the hallway to the bathroom.

Liv refused to look toward her father's bedroom. It could only start the tears flowing all over again. She'd cried enough for one day. With cattle in danger of a wolf attack, she couldn't spare the time and emotional energy it sapped out of her.

Hawkeye's strong arms around her had stemmed the last flow. She couldn't rely on him to be there to hold her every time she thought about her father and the fact she had no family left.

"Abe is family," she reminded herself aloud as she stepped into the bathroom and closed the door behind her.

A few minutes later, she stood beneath the shower, dark streaks of water making trails down the drain. Liv wondered if Hawkeye had found the shower in the barn or if he would wait until she finished before washing the dirt off his body. She also wondered what it would be like to share a shower with the man.

Her belly tightened and an ache grew between her thighs. How long had it been since a man had held her in his arms? She'd been too wrapped up in her studies in college to date much. And most of the boys hadn't been interested in intellectual conversations. They'd wanted only one thing. Now that she'd kissed the ruggedly handsome army ranger, Liv could understand fixating on getting naked with another person.

Standing beneath the warm water sluicing over her shoulders, she could imagine Hawkeye sharing the space with her, his broad shoulders filling the shower. She tried to tell herself it was wrong to think about him naked, but it beat the heck out of thinking about her grief.

So, standing naked in the shower spray, Liv let her thoughts go to the ranger and something inside blossomed and grew more intense, spreading all the way out to her fingertips.

She closed her eyes and imagined the man lathering the bar of soap and slathering it along the column of her throat, over the swells of her breasts and down her torso to the juncture of her thighs. She gasped and turned toward the spray, her breathing ragged, her blood on fire and pumping hard and fast through her veins.

Reaching down, she turned the handle, reducing the heat until cool water chilled her skin. But nothing could quench the flames raging inside.

At last, she shut off the water, reached for a towel and dried herself quickly. The sooner she dressed, the sooner she'd stop thinking of Hawkeye naked.

Or so she thought. Wearing clean jeans, thick socks, cowboy boots and the sweatshirt, she assumed any lusty inclinations would be thoroughly squelched. Not so. She'd forgone wearing a bra, reasoning the sweatshirt was enough. Only the inside of the shirt brushed against her nipples, making them bead into tight little nubs.

Having been gone from the herd long enough, Liv threw on a jacket and hurried through the house and out onto the porch. Then she thought about the shower in the barn. How long had it been since someone had taken fresh towels out there? She ran back inside to the linen closet, retrieved a large, fluffy towel and returned to the barn.

She listened for the sounds of wolves or livestock in distress. Silence reigned, except for the chirping of crickets and the occasional owl hooting in the distance.

Hawkeye was nowhere to be seen.

For a moment, Liv panicked. Had he left? She spun to find his truck sitting where he'd parked it. Relief washed over her and she entered the barn, going to the tack room that doubled as the foreman's office. Her father had installed a shower at the rear of the tack room on her mother's insistence. She wouldn't let him into the house while he was covered in dust, claiming he left a muddy trail when he did. Rather than hose down in the yard, he'd built the shower, complete with a small hot water heater. It had saved him from a freezing shower on more than one occasion.

Outside the bathroom door, Liv paused, listening for the sound of the water hitting the stall doors and floor, verifying that Hawkeye was inside, probably naked, his hands and body covered in soapsuds.

Liv raised her hand to knock, thought better of it and lowered it. He wouldn't hear her knock, and if he did, he might slip on the bathroom floor trying to get to the door.

Liv figured there wouldn't be any clean towels in the bathroom, which meant Hawkeye would have to drip dry unless she could get the towel to him before he finished his shower.

If the door wasn't locked, she could slip in, drop the towel on the counter and exit with Hawkeye none the wiser.

She twisted the handle and the door opened.

Her heart hammering against her ribs, Liv eased into the small room, laid the towel on the counter and turned to leave.

That was when she noticed the sheerness of the shower curtain and the explicitly defined silhouette of Hawkeye's form behind the milk-white, plastic sheath.

Liv froze, her gaze raking over the thick forearms and biceps, the narrow waist and the thighs. Sweet heaven, the man was built like a gladiator, all muscles and sinew from his thick neck to his tight, well-defined calves.

The water ceased spraying and the curtain jerked back. Hawkeye stared out at her, a quirky smile curling the corners of his mouth. "Like what you see?"

For half a second, she froze, her gaze not connecting with his eyes, but running the length of his lean, sexy body all the way down to his…

Liv jerked her eyes back up to connect with his, red-hot heat rising up her neck into her cheeks, burning its way out to her ears. "A towel," she blathered. "I brought you a towel."

Still her flight instinct wouldn't kick in.

"Thank you. I'd anticipated dripping dry." He stepped out on the cool tile floor, his grin spreading as he reached for the towel. "Are you going to help me dry off?"

"No. I…uh…was just leaving." Finally, her legs moved and she ran out the door, slamming it behind her. She would have run all the way out to the barnyard, but the horse in the stall whinnied, the sound just loud enough to penetrate her quivering brain cells.

Stormy, her gray quarter-horse gelding, pawed at the stall door, bringing her focus to the animal anxious to get her attention. She remembered then that he hadn't been fed that evening. Abe usually performed all of the chores before supper. His hunger and the nervous energy from the ruckus outside made for an unhappy horse. And he wasn't the only one.

Three other horses were stabled in the barn, all stamping their hooves, ready for hay and grain.

Liv had to suck up her embarrassment and get to work feeding the animals. They didn't have to suffer because she'd made a fool of herself.

She scooped a couple of coffee cans full of sweet feed and dumped them into buckets.

Stormy whickered again.

"I hear you. You'll get yours first, since you're the loudest." She carried the bucket to the stall and hefted it over the top, hanging it on the hook on the other side. Stormy immediately buried his nose in the feed and quieted down.

"How much hay do you give each?" Hawkeye's voice made her jump.

Pulling herself together, she turned with as much dignity as she could muster after seeing the man completely naked. "A section each." As her gaze met his, heat rushed up into her cheeks. She ducked her head and hurried over to the next stall, hanging the second bucket over the side. The bay mare in the stall nodded her head as if in approval and dug into her meal.

One more trip to the feed bins and she was finished with the sweet feed.

Hawkeye had placed sections of hay in all of the occupied stalls and started filling water troughs.

Liv took a deep breath and launched into sleeping arrangements. "You can have the spare bedroom in the house. It has clean sheets on the bed."

"We've already discussed this. I'm staying outside with you."

"I'll have my gun, and I'll build a fire," she said. "I've done it before." She gave him a tight smile. "I'm not afraid of the dark."

"Not alone," he repeated. "I'll bed down outside with you." He finished filling the troughs.

Liv turned off the water and wiped her hands on her jeans. "I'll get some firewood and tinder."

"Do you mind if I break up a bale of hay for a pallet?"

"Knock yourself out." Liv hurried to the stack of wood her father and Abe had cut for the huge fireplace in the house. She selected three logs and some kindling and hurried back to the barnyard close to the pasture fence where the cattle had settled in for the night.

The sky had turned black, the stars and moon illuminating the landscape enough that

Liv didn't need a flashlight to see. She made another trip for more logs and dropped them beside the first load. "I'll be back."

Liv returned to the house. This time her mind was on the man she'd be lying beside under the blanket of stars. The ache of memories wasn't quite as powerful when she entered through the kitchen. She was able to retrieve the sleeping bag from the closet and get out without shedding another tear. Liv considered that a significant accomplishment.

In the couple of minutes it took Liv to get her bag, Hawkeye had arranged a straw pallet by the fence, spread a sleeping bag over it and was in the process of starting a fire.

"Well, you're a regular Boy Scout," she commented as she laid her bag on the ground nearby and sat cross-legged. "Did you rub two sticks together to get that started?"

"I found matches in the desk in the tack room." He blew a steady stream of air onto the flaming tinder to get the fire burning brightly. In a few minutes, the flames climbed onto the logs and Hawkeye sat back.

He frowned when he turned toward her. "I put the hay out for both of us. No use sleeping on the hard ground."

She shrugged, not wanting to get too close to him. Whenever she did, sparks flew. Not the mad and angry kind, but the lusty, sexy ones. "I'm fine where I am."

"Look, I promise not to touch you." His lips quirked into a smile. "Unless you want me to."

She wasn't so worried about him touching *her*, as she was about her own desire to touch *him*. But she would get little sleep on the hard ground. Liv picked up her sleeping bag and spread it out next to Hawkeye's on the side closest to the fire. Her pulse quickened and her insides heated. She sat on the bag and raised her hand to the warm fire, glad for the sweatshirt and jacket. The temperature would dive to near freezing by morning.

Rather than stare at him, she shifted her gaze to the silhouettes of the cattle in the pasture. "Any more signs of the wolves?"

"None. And the livestock have settled in for the night. You don't have to sleep out here, if you don't want to. I can keep an eye on the herd."

"Thanks. But I don't want to rely on anyone. If I'm going to stay, I need to be able to handle things on my own when the need calls for it."

"If?" He sat beside her, staring into the fire. "Was there any question of your staying?"

She wrapped her arms around her legs and rested her head on her knees. "The ranch doesn't feel right without my dad."

"I take it you grew up here?"

She tipped her head toward her home. "My mother gave birth to me on this ranch. They couldn't get to the hospital in time, so my father delivered me in the house he built for her." She smiled, staring into the fire, the few memories of her mother crowding into her thoughts. "She was pretty, with blond hair and blue eyes. I don't look anything like her. I get my red hair and green eyes from my dad."

"Where is your mother?"

Liv sighed. Her chest tightened. Even though her mother had been gone a long time, she still missed her. "She died of a cancer when I was twelve."

For a long moment Hawkeye remained quiet. "I'm sorry. It had to be rough on you as a little girl."

"Yeah. I didn't have her around for a lot of things girls share with their mothers. But my father tried to make up for it." She laughed and nearly choked on a sob. "He even learned to French braid my hair. He was determined to be a great father and a substitute mother all wrapped up in one person."

"And run a ranch."

"Thankfully, I wasn't much of a girlie-girl to begin with. I loved ranching as much as my father."

"But you lived in Seattle for how long?"

"Seven years. Through college and three years following."

"Why didn't you come back after college?"

"My father made me promise to give city life a shot before coming home to Grizzly Pass. I was three years into the five years when I got the call." Again, her throat tightened, threatening to cut off her air.

Hawkeye slipped an arm around her waist and pulled her up against him.

"You said you wouldn't touch me," she said, though she didn't push him away. It felt good to have someone to lean on, especially when the main man in her life couldn't be there anymore.

"I said I wouldn't unless you wanted me to." His arm tightened around her waist. "I figured you could use a shoulder to lean on about now."

"Thanks." She leaned her head into the crook

of his arm and inhaled the woodsy, smoky scent of a man used to the outdoors.

"So that leaves you and Abe to run the ranch. Wouldn't it be easier just to sell it?"

She stiffened. "That's what Mr. Rausch tried to tell me. I'll be damned if I fire-sale this place to him. He owns enough of Grizzly Pass without owning my family ranch. Besides, he'd probably turn it into a big-game-hunting place where they raise prize elk and buffalo for rich folks to come slaughter as they stand at the feeders." Liv shook her head. "I can't let that happen."

"I take it you have a job in Seattle. Won't they expect you to come back to work soon?"

She nodded. "I took a leave of absence. I haven't completely quit."

"Do you want to go back?" Hawkeye asked.

She shrugged. "For the past seven years, all I wanted was to come home to Grizzly Pass and Stone Oak Ranch."

"And now?"

She leaned into him, glad for his warmth and strength. "I don't know. I'm having a hard time imagining this place without my dad." Liv's eyes stung with ready tears every time she thought of her father. "I don't know," she whispered past the knot around her vocal cords.

"Well, for a little while you won't have to make that decision. While I'm here, I'll help with chores, feeding and taking care of the livestock. But you should consider hiring more help."

"I know. CJ won't be around all the time and I need full-time help." She lifted her head and looked up at his face. "Enough about me. My life right now is too depressing. Tell me about you."

HAWKEYE SHRUGGED. "THERE'S not much to tell." He didn't like talking about himself. Most of his recent memories were of war and fighting. Coming back to the States had left him feeling itchy and uncomfortable. But in the grand scheme of world events, his feelings didn't amount to a hill of beans.

"Where did you grow up?" Olivia persisted.

Knowing the woman wouldn't give up unless he gave her a little of his background, he sighed. "On a ranch in the Texas Panhandle."

"See? That didn't hurt so much, now, did it?" She shifted her gaze back to the fire. "I should have known. You were right at home, feeding animals. Did your family own the ranch?"

Here was the huge difference between Hawkeye and Olivia. He was from humbler beginnings. His family never owned any acreage. Especially not in the magnitude of what Olivia's father owned. "My father was the foreman. My mother helped out as the cook in the ranch house."

"They must have been great role models. After living in the city where most people have never been up close and personal with a horse or a cow, it made me appreciate all of the hard work Abe and my father put into this place." She snuggled closer. "Is it me, or is it getting colder?"

"Colder," Hawkeye said, his side warming where she pressed against it. She fit perfectly under his arm. He had to fight the urge to kiss her temple.

"I assume you ride," she said, her voice soft in the darkness.

"Four-wheelers."

Again, Olivia glanced up at him. "You can't tell me you grew up on a ranch in Texas and never learned to ride. I won't believe it."

Hawkeye pressed his lips together, memories

flooding into his head. "My sister and I learned to ride bareback before we learned to walk. I did a little junior rodeoing, but not for long."

"But you don't ride now?" The starlight and the three-quarter moon reflected off her eyes, making them sparkling diamonds in the night.

"No," he said. "I don't ride now."

When she opened her mouth to ask why, he shook his head. "Please. Don't ask."

She closed her mouth, her gaze scanning his face, as if searching for clues. Finally, she looked back to the fire. "I always wanted a sibling." Olivia sighed. "My parents tried for more children, but it just didn't happen. I think my father would have liked a boy to take hunting and fishing."

Off the subject of horseback riding, Hawkeye relaxed and let the warmth of the fire and the flickering flames calm him. "I can't imagine you staying home. Surely you went with him?"

Olivia chuckled. "Much to my mother's chagrin, I tagged along with my father, dressed in camouflage or hunter orange. She couldn't get me into a dress except on Sundays. I got my first deer when I was nine."

"I bet your dad was just as proud of you, even if you weren't a boy."

"I know he was. But my parents would have liked more children. It made my mother sad that she couldn't get pregnant again." Olivia yawned. "Tell me about your family."

Again, Hawkeye tensed. "Do you always talk this much?"

Olivia yawned again. "Only when I'm trying to stay awake at the same time as I'm trying not to think about my dad and the fact he isn't coming home ever again."

Hawkeye's chest tightened. He knew what it was like to lose someone you cared about. Yes, his parents were alive and still lived on the ranch in Texas. But he'd lost a number of friends in the war. Friends he considered his brothers. And then there was Sarah.

"What is your sister like?"

The dull ache that had been with him most of his life intensified.

"Sarah was everything I wasn't—pretty, delicate, blond-haired and blue-eyed like my mother. She laughed all the time. Life was a joy to her, and she was a joy to everyone whose life she touched."

Olivia rested her hand on his and squeezed. "What happened to her?"

The horror of that day replayed in Hawkeye's mind like a video. "Sarah loved riding her horse, Socks. We raced often, thundering across the pasture toward the barn or to our favorite swimming hole. On her birthday, we were racing. Her horse wasn't quite as fast as mine, so I slowed to let her win, to make her day even more special. Socks galloped ahead. They went down into a gully and, on their way back up, Socks reared unexpectedly. Sarah was thrown. She landed on her head, snapping her neck. She died instantly."

"How old was she?"

"Ten."

"And you?" Her hand tightened on his.

"Fifteen. Almost sixteen."

"Wow. I imagine that was hard on you."

He'd jumped off his horse and run to his sister, but nothing he could have done would have changed the outcome. The two horses were spooked and took off back to the barn. Hawkeye had been torn between staying with his sister and going for help. Finally, he'd left her and run all the way back to the house to get his father.

"Sarah was everything to my parents," he said softly.

His mother had ridden in the truck beside his

father all the way back to where Sarah lay. For a few minutes, Hawkeye hadn't been able to remember exactly where she'd been. When they finally found her, her face had been pale, the light drained out of a bright and happy human being.

"I'm sorry," Olivia said. "I would like to have met her. She sounds like she was amazing."

"She was." Hawkeye didn't pull his hand free of Olivia's. Her touch seemed to ease the pain he'd lived with for so long.

"You felt responsible, didn't you?" Olivia said.

"As an adult, I can reason with myself, but I still come back to the same 'if only' scenarios," he said.

"What do you mean?"

"If only we hadn't gone riding that day, she'd still be with us."

"You don't know that," Olivia countered.

"If only I hadn't challenged her to that race."

Olivia's hand stroked his. "Are you sure she didn't challenge you?"

"Even if she did, I didn't have to take her up on the challenge." A number of times Hawkeye had wished he could go back and do that entire day over. Anything to get Sarah back.

Olivia turned in his arms. "So you stopped riding horses to punish yourself?"

"It's more complicated." Hawkeye stared off at the bright moon rising above the mountaintops. "My mother was devastated by Sarah's death. She quit caring about anything, stopped eating and sank into a deep depression. My father had a job to do. He couldn't stay at home and take care of her."

"You were her only other child?"

Hawkeye nodded. "I never knew someone could be that depressed or how debilitating it could be. I'd lost my sister, but I was losing my mother, too. So I promised her I'd never ride again."

"And you felt like it was all your fault."

"Yeah." He looked at her for a moment and then back at the moon.

"Looking back, I'm sure you realize it wasn't."

He nodded. "But I was older than Sarah. I should have done something to prevent it from happening."

"Like?"

He shook his head. "I tell myself that I should have stayed at home. Then Sarah wouldn't have been on that horse to begin with."

"Should have, could have, would have, doesn't change anything." Olivia touched his cheek with her fingers.

Hawkeye leaned into her palm. "I know."

"You did everything you could have done."

"Except save her."

"I'm sorry," Olivia repeated and leaned up, pressing her lips to his.

He raised his arms around her and held her tightly against his body, his mouth crashing down on hers. God, he wanted this woman who'd lost her father so recently. She needed the shoulder to lean on more than Hawkeye. Instead she gave him the opportunity to share his deepest regrets, offering her sympathy for his loss from over sixteen years ago.

Olivia deserved to mourn her father, not listen to his sad story. Hawkeye gripped her arms, pressed Liv away from him and dropped his hands to his sides. "We should get some sleep. Tomorrow could prove as challenging as today."

"Nothing could be as challenging as burying your father," she whispered.

She was probably right. But Hawkeye's current challenge was to keep from taking this woman he'd only met a few hours ago and making sweet love to her under the star-filled sky.

Olivia stared up into his eyes, her own glazed, her lips swollen from his kiss.

Rather than kiss her again and compound his error, Hawkeye turned away, closed his eyes and listened for sounds of wolves or mooing cattle. Silence soothed the darkness, marred only by the occasional hoot of an owl.

Hawkeye lay on his side, facing away from Olivia, making it clear he didn't want to interfere in her space or she in his, though interfering was all he could think about.

Eventually, she settled behind him, leaving him in silence, with his burgeoning desire keeping him awake into the small hours of the morning. This mission could prove to be one of the hardest he'd ever undertaken, if he planned to keep his hands off the pretty ranch owner.

Chapter Six

Liv lay very still for a long time after that kiss.

That kiss.

Never in all her twenty-five years had she had a kiss that left her as shaken and as hungry for more. Liv liked being in control of her life, her emotions and her destiny. In one kiss, Hawkeye had shown her just how out of control her heart could be.

She lay staring up at the stars and the moon well into the night. When she finally fell asleep, she dreamed of lying naked with Hawkeye in a soft bed, his arms wrapped around her from behind, his lips nuzzling the sensitive skin of her neck.

Liv woke with a start, forcing herself out of the dream. He'd made it clear he didn't need her kisses by breaking it off and turning away.

Why would she dream about him holding her when it wasn't going to happen? He was there as part of his job. She was a means to an end, giving him access to her property to look out for whoever might have killed her father or was stirring up trouble in the area.

Liv blinked her eyes up at the stars. The chill night air cooled her face, but not her body snuggly wrapped in the sleeping bag. Though the sleeping bag was considerably heavier than usual. She shifted onto her back, only to realize the bag wasn't what was heavy.

Hawkeye's arm lay across her middle, tucked beneath her breasts. He'd spooned her body with his, sharing his warmth.

Liv smiled. Yeah, he could turn off his desire, but he must have felt something or he wouldn't have snuggled up to her in the night, laying his arm across her to keep her warm.

Rolling back to her side, she pressed her back to Hawkeye's front and nestled in his embrace, her eyes drifting closed again. Morning would come soon, and with it, she'd be forced to sort out her feelings and get on with the task of taking care of a ranch. But for now, she had the strength of Hawkeye's arm and body beside her. That was enough to get her through the night.

As the first hint of morning lightened the sky, Liv woke, strangely pleased that Hawkeye's arm was still around her, his body pressed firmly to her back. Feeling a little on the shy side, she inched her way from beneath that arm and rolled herself and her sleeping bag away from him before sitting up.

Hawkeye slept on, his chest rising and falling in a steady pattern.

In the gray light of dawn, Liv studied his face, softened by slumber. Tanned and rugged, Hawkeye appeared more gentle and vulnerable in his sleep. With his eyes closed, his long, dark lashes made shadowy crescents on his cheeks. Any woman would give her eye teeth for lashes like that. Hawkeye would sire beautiful children with his dark hair and blue eyes.

Liv's chest tightened. She'd always imagined herself having kids, even dreamed about them. Somehow, she'd never pictured the face of a husband in the dreams. Perhaps because she hadn't met Hawkeye.

Now she could imagine dreaming about a man with dark hair and blue eyes and a little girl of the same coloring.

Holy hell, what was she thinking? Hawkeye wasn't going to be there after the mystery of her father's death was resolved and the people responsible for the troubles in the area were revealed.

She stared at his rugged face for a while longer, attracted to the rough stubble on his chin and the fullness of his lips. Before she could think her way out of doing it, she leaned over and brushed those lips with her own.

When she realized what she'd done, she held her breath, fully expecting his eyes to open. They didn't, and his breathing continued slow and steady. Liv let go of the breath she held and rose to her feet. She had a lot of things to do that day and kissing a sleeping man wasn't one of them.

For a moment, she thought his eyes opened slightly, but he didn't move from his original position.

Quickly, before she changed her mind and slipped back beneath his arm, Liv ran for the house, up the steps and into the home she'd grown up in.

With light edging through the windows, Liv was able to make her way to the bathroom without flipping any electrical switches. Once in the bathroom, she closed the door and leaned against it, willing her breathing to return to normal. Who was she running from, anyway? Not Hawkeye. He hadn't come after her. And it wasn't Hawkeye she was afraid of. He'd been there for her by saving Abe from a flaming truck and her from a stampede. Then why had she run all the way up to the house?

If she was being honest with herself, she'd admit she was afraid of the way she was feeling toward the man she'd only met the day before. Was she subconsciously clinging to him because of the loss of her father? Was Hawkeye the father figure she wished she hadn't lost?

Her lips tingled at the memory of the kisses.

Liv smothered a nervous laugh. No way in hell a kiss like the one last night was fatherly. She didn't think of Hawkeye as a father figure. Far from it. Her body burned with the warmth she'd felt with her back pressed against his front even with the thickness of two sleeping bags between them.

Dragging in a deep, steadying breath, she pushed away from the door, splashed water on her face, brushed her teeth and pulled her hair back into a neat ponytail. Feeling a little more in control of herself and her situation, she peeked out into the hallway, half expecting to see Hawkeye waiting outside.

Disappointment flashed through her. Apparently, she was the only one thinking about the other person in this case. Hawkeye was probably sound asleep on the ground outside where she'd left him, not a single thought about her floating through his dreams.

Shoving her sleeves up her arms, she marched into the kitchen and started breakfast. God, she hated cooking. Her father and Abe had alternated kitchen duties. When Liv was home, they continued their routine and she helped out by washing dishes, cleaning the house and bathrooms as well as taking care of the livestock.

Cooking was not her strong suit. She burned everything.

Well, not today.

She dug the frying pans out of the cabinet and bacon and eggs from the refrigerator. Soon she had bacon popping in the frying pan and had poured eight scrambled eggs into another skillet.

"I've got this." Her confidence growing, she reached for the loaf of bread and popped four slices into the toaster. Then she thought about the coffee that she should have started brewing before anything else. Turning her attention to the coffeemaker, she poured several scoops of grounds into the filter and dumped a carafe of water over it.

By the time she turned back to the stovetop, smoke was roiling from the bacon pan.

"Shoot! Shoot! Shoot!" She ripped the pan from the fire. Hot bacon grease sloshed onto her hand. Liv let loose a string of curses, slammed the pan back on the stove and dived for the sink, her hand stinging where the grease had landed.

"Need some help?"

"No," she responded automatically. She turned on the cold water and jammed her hand beneath it.

Hawkeye trotted across the kitchen and turned off the burner beneath the smoking bacon. "Do you always burn the kitchen down when you cook breakfast?"

"No," she said, her voice a little harsh, the pain diminishing as the grease was removed from her skin. No doubt, she'd have a blister there. "Well, yes, actually. I'm a bit hopeless as a cook."

"And you lived on your own for how many years?"

"Long enough to figure out a microwave and frozen dinners."

"For breakfast?" Hawkeye pushed a spatula through the scrambled eggs and raised his brows when the eggs stuck to the bottom of the pan. "We might want to start over."

Liv inhaled and let go of a deep breath, her eyes stinging. "Abe and my father were in charge of cooking. The only culinary delights I ever managed were hot dogs on the grill." She stared down at the red spot on her hand. "And I can make a decent cup of coffee."

"At least you have your priorities straight. How about you butter the toast and pour us a cup of coffee while I scrape these eggs out of the pan and put on a fresh batch?"

"I really had every intention of having a decent breakfast on the table. I figured, since I'm getting your services free, the least I could do was provide decent meals." She sighed. "I'm sorry."

"Don't be. Not everyone is born with the knack for cooking."

"Sometimes I wish I was more like my mother. She was a wonderful cook."

"I'm sure you made up for it in other ways."

Liv nodded. "I'm pretty good at everything to do with ranching."

"There you go." He finished cleaning the

pan, dropped butter to melt across the slick surface and cracked nine eggs onto it. Soon he was scooping fluffy yellow eggs onto three plates, adding the salvaged bacon and buttered toast.

Liv sat at the table, thankful for Hawkeye's sure hand at cooking and the hot steaming cup of java in her hand. "Three plates?"

"CJ should be here anytime."

A knock on the front door of the house made Liv start.

Before Liv could rise from her chair, Hawkeye held up a hand. "Stay. I'll get it."

Liv sank back down and lifted her fork, pretending interest in the light and fluffy eggs Hawkeye had whipped up, when in fact she was more attuned to the way his hips swayed in the faded blue jeans he wore.

Liv's pulse quickened. She had to force her gaze back to her plate full of scrambled eggs and slightly burned bacon.

A few moments later, CJ entered the room, a battered straw cowboy hat in his hand, a ruddy pink flush building in his dark-skinned cheeks. His raven hair was shaggy, hanging down around his ears and on his collar, like he hadn't had a haircut in a month or two. "Sorry to bother you at breakfast, Miss Dawson."

"Not at all. In fact, I believe Mr. Walsh made enough breakfast for you. Have a seat."

He straightened. "I'm here to work, ma'am. If you could tell me where to start, I'll get to it."

Liv shook her head. "You can start at the breakfast table and load up on enough protein to keep you working hard through the day. Then you can do the dishes."

CJ shot a glance at Hawkeye.

"She's the boss. I'd do what she says." When CJ glanced back at Liv, Hawkeye winked.

"I don't feel right eating your food. I came to work."

"I understand. But I plan on leaving you here while I go to town for feed and supplies. I need to know you won't pass out because you haven't had a decent meal."

"I won't pass out." The teen stood tall, his shoulders back. "I'm strong."

Hawkeye pulled out the chair in front of his untouched plate of food and pressed CJ into it. "Eat, or we'll never hear the end of it."

Liv ducked her head to hide the smile pulling at her lips.

Hawkeye retrieved the third plate and sat in the seat beside CJ.

Soon they were all tucking into a hearty breakfast.

When Liv had almost cleaned her plate she caught Hawkeye's gaze.

"What's this about going into town?" he asked.

"I need to replace the feed and supplies we lost in the crash yesterday. We're down to the bottom of the grain barrel for the horses and I need barbed wire and staples for the fence repairs we'll be doing later." She drew in a deep breath.

"Which brings us to the question of transportation," Hawkeye said. "Do you have another ranch truck?"

Liv shook her head. "Sorry, that old truck was the only one we had. I'll have to find a good used one to replace it. But that will take some searching. In the meantime, I can use my SUV. It'll carry the bags of feed and barbed wire."

Hawkeye shook his head. "We'll take my truck."

"I don't want to take advantage of you and your truck. Ranching can be harsh on vehicles."

"I bought it to be a work truck."

"Yeah, but—"

"We'll take my truck."

Liv wasn't sure she liked being overruled on her own ranch, but it would be easier to load and unload fifty-pound bags of feed into an open pickup bed than to slide them in and out of the back of her SUV. She'd have to search the internet that night to find a good used four-wheel-drive pickup. Winters in Wyoming could be harsh, cold and snowy. Whatever she got had to be able to climb slippery dirt roads in all weather conditions.

"Okay." She pushed back from the table and focused on her new hired hand. "CJ, are you ready to learn the ropes?"

He set his fork on his plate. "Yes, ma'am. But I need to do the dishes."

"You could do them at noon when you come inside to make a sandwich for lunch. Right now, I want to show you what needs to be done so that I can get into town and back before it gets late."

"Yes, ma'am." CJ piled his plate on Liv's and Hawkeye's and carried them to the sink. Then he hurried for the back door, opened it and held it for Liv.

She smiled as she walked out onto the porch. If the teen worked as hard at doing his chores right as he worked at being polite, he'd be a real asset to the ranch in Abe's absence.

After showing CJ what stalls needed to be cleaned and which horses needed to be exercised and fed, she left the teen, grabbed her purse and climbed into the passenger seat of Hawkeye's truck. "Do you think he'll be all right?"

"He seems to know his way around livestock." Hawkeye shifted into Reverse, backed up and turned the truck around. "He'll be fine."

"We won't be gone long," Liv reasoned. "Hopefully we'll be back before lunch."

"I'm counting on it. I want to get out to check on the downed fences."

Liv snorted. "You and me both. Cows seem to know when a fence is down and are drawn to the holes like magnets."

Hawkeye nodded. "I remember. My father worked on a ten-thousand-acre ranch in Texas. A tree could fall on the farthest fence in the most remote corner of the property and the cattle would find it, exit and wander onto another rancher's land. Thankfully, all of the steers were tagged for just that reason. We were forever trading livestock with the neighbors."

Liv smiled. "We have the added complication of grazing cattle on government land. Just *finding* your animals can be a challenge. We train them to come to the honking of a horn."

"Seems to be a universal cattle call." Hawkeye glanced across at her. "With your father gone, are you sure you want to take over the reins of a cattle ranch on your own?"

Liv stared out the window, her heart tightening in her chest. She was hit all over again that her father wouldn't be coming home to handle the myriad problems that came up on a daily basis when managing a cattle ranch.

"All the years I've been away from home, I dreamed of returning and helping my father with the ranch. I love working with the animals, riding horses and getting dirty." She gave him a sheepish grin. "I guess you've noticed I'm not much of a girlie-girl."

Hawkeye's gaze connected with hers, the heat in his look warming Liv all over. "I hadn't noticed. To me, you're all female. Through and through. With the added advantage…you aren't squeamish and you aren't afraid of anything."

Liv dragged her gaze away from his, afraid

shc would lose herself in it. "Most men would find that intimidating."

"Then most men are fools."

She looked back in time to see Hawkeye's lips quirk upward. "As an army ranger, I take it you aren't intimidated by much?"

"Oh, I wouldn't say that. I can be scared by a howitzer if it's pointed directly at me."

Liv nodded. "That would have me shaking in my boots. Have you had a howitzer pointed at you?"

"No, but I've had a live machine gun pointed at me and my team, and explosives detonate within ten feet of where I was standing." His words faded into silence.

Liv's chest tightened again. All the while she'd been mourning her father's death, she hadn't stopped to consider Hawkeye's losses. Yeah, he'd lost his little sister a long time ago, but what about more recently? "Do you miss your work with the army?"

He nodded. "I miss the men who were part of my team."

She lowered her voice and asked, "Were they also the target of that machine gun?"

For a long moment, he remained silent.

Liv thought he preferred to avoid the question altogether. She turned toward the road ahead, accepting that he had a right to his silence.

"Yes. But it was the grenade that went off in the middle of them that did the most damage. I lost my battle buddy that day."

Liv's eyes stung at the hollowness in Hawkeye's tone. She swallowed hard and remained silent for a full minute before responding. "I'm sorry. He must have meant a lot to you."

His lips pressed together. "Mac was the brother I never had. We'd been through a lot together. He had my back."

And Liv would bet Hawkeye blamed himself for not protecting his buddy, like he'd blamed himself for not saving his sister. Her heart hurt for Hawkeye.

"If you're like me," Liv said, "you wander around in a bit of a haze, wondering if he'd still be here if you'd done something different. I keep wondering if I'd broken my promise to my father and come home when I'd wanted, would he still be alive?"

"You can't undo what's done. No amount of what-ifs will bring them back," Hawkeye said, his tone harsh, his jaw tight.

"I know that, but it doesn't stop my mind

from going through alternate endings." Liv pushed the loose hairs out of her face, tucking them behind her ears. "It's hard for me to think of life without my father in it. I keep thinking it's all a bad dream and I'll wake up to find him out in the barn, mucking a stall, or sitting in his lounge chair watching his favorite team play football."

"I keep thinking I'll get a text from Mac asking where the hell I am. Why am I not at the gym working out, or eating pizza with the team?" Hawkeye's grip tightened on the steering wheel until his knuckles turned white.

About that time, they arrived on the edge of town.

"Sheriff Scott said my truck would be towed to Roy Taylor's body shop in town. I'd like to stop by and see if any of the feed bags that were in the back of the truck are still intact."

"Point the way," Hawkeye said.

"Right turn at the next street."

Hawkeye turned where she'd indicated and pulled into the gravel parking lot of the body shop.

The damaged truck was parked at the side of the building, the front end smashed with clumps of dirt clinging to the fenders.

Liv hopped out of the passenger seat and hurried over to the truck. As she suspected, the bags of feed had been thrown clear of the truck or were busted, with grain scattered across the truck bed. Not one of the bags were salvageable. And the roll of barbed wire was missing.

"Hey, Liv." A man walked out of the open overhead door, wiping his hands on a greasy rag.

"Hi, Roy." She nodded toward the truck. "Any chance you can fix her?"

He shook his head. "I'm afraid it'll cost more than the truck is worth. Do you have collision coverage on it?"

Liv shrugged. "Knowing my father and how old that truck is, I'm betting he only had liability insurance coverage."

Roy tipped his head. "It's up to you, but if it were me, I'd haul it off to the junkyard for scrap and find a newer truck."

Liv nodded. "I'd come to the same conclusion, but it's good to know you agree."

"Sorry about your father. He was a good man." Roy dipped his head. "I'll take care of hauling your truck off to the junkyard."

"Send the tow-truck bill to me. I'll make sure it gets paid," Liv said.

"No charge. Your dad helped me out on several occasions."

"Thanks, Roy." She hugged him, fighting back unwanted tears, and hurried back to Hawkeye's truck. She jumped in and stared straight ahead.

Hawkeye slid behind the wheel and twisted the key. The engine leaped to life, but he paused before shifting into gear. "Everything all right?"

"Yes. Just go." She leaned her head back and closed her eyes, a teardrop escaping as she did. "Why does everything have to remind me of him?"

"This is a small town. Every life touches another."

She gave a shaky sigh. "And the only way to get away from that is to leave. What if I'm not ready to leave?"

Chapter Seven

Hawkeye shifted into gear and pulled out of the parking lot of the body shop. He knew exactly what Olivia was going through. When he'd recovered enough to return to the apartment complex where he and Mac had lived, he'd been haunted by every little reminder of his friend.

No sooner had Mac's parents moved his things out of his apartment than another tenant moved in. Hawkeye had wanted to pound on the door and tell them to get out. Mac was supposed to live there. When he went to the gym on post, people would stop and ask about Mac. People who didn't know Mac hadn't made it back from the war. It was all Hawkeye could do not to slug one of them in the face. Not because they were being disrespectful. But because they were alive and Mac wasn't.

He'd jumped at the opportunity to leave everything he knew in order to get away from the memories of Mac and the other members of his team he'd lost in that last firefight. Far from Fort Bragg, far from his unit and his life as an army ranger, he'd hoped to get his life back on track.

Instead he was paired with a woman who'd lost her father and was in the first stages of grief. What did he have to offer her when he couldn't get his own life together?

"Where to?" he asked. The sixty-four-million-dollar question he'd yet to answer. Where was he going?

Olivia had the answer, even if he didn't. "The feed store."

Hawkeye pulled onto Main Street and drove down to the only feed store in town. He backed into the loading dock at the front of the store.

A small crowd had gathered around the raised front porch of the store, and a white van displaying a local news station logo on the side was parked nearby. A man was setting up a camera on a tripod, aiming it at the porch of the feed store.

"What's going on?" Hawkeye asked.

"Because the feed-store porch makes a great raised stage, any town meeting or political campaigning is usually conducted here. Based on the placards leaning against the porch, I'd say a political candidate is about to give a speech." She pushed open her door. "We'd better get our feed and get out before we are surrounded by spectators."

Hawkeye dropped down from the truck and followed Olivia up the steps and into the feed store.

People milled around, pretending to shop for tack and horse liniment. Hawkeye suspected they were waiting for the show to begin.

Olivia made for the counter and waited her turn in line. Once there, she placed her order for feed, staples and a roll of barbed wire.

The man behind the counter rang up her purchases and took her credit card. When he handed it back with the slip for her to sign, he said, "Sorry about what happened to your father, Liv."

"Thanks, Mr. Nelson." Olivia signed the slip and replaced her card in her wallet.

"Don!" Mr. Nelson held up the printout of Olivia's purchases. "Help Miss Dawson with her order."

A big man with heavy brows and a deep tan emerged from a back room, snatched the paper from Mr. Nelson, shot a narrow-eyed glare at Olivia and walked back into what appeared to be a warehouse in the back of the main store. A few minutes later, he wheeled out a cart loaded with eight bags of feed, a bucket of staples and a roll of barbed wire. He headed straight for the loading dock without saying a word to Olivia.

Hawkeye studied the man. Something about his bearing gave him away as prior military. As he loaded the bags of feed into the back of the truck, Hawkeye noticed the tattoos on the man's arm. One was a US Marine Corps symbol with a skull and crossbones positioned above it.

When the man finished loading the supplies into the truck he turned to leave.

Hawkeye stuck out his hand. "Name's Trace Walsh. I notice you have a Marine Corps tattoo. Prior service?"

The man looked sideways at Hawkeye through narrowed eyes and didn't take the proffered hand. "Yeah. What's it to you?"

"It's just nice to meet another veteran. I'm army."

The man's lip curled into a sneer. "Yeah, well, I have work to do."

"I'm sorry but I didn't catch your name," Hawkeye persisted.

"Sweeney. Not that it's any of your business." He turned and left them standing on the dock.

Hawkeye nodded toward the retreating man. "Someone you know?"

Olivia shook her head. "He looks older than me. I don't remember him from high school. However, I do recognize his name. The Sweeneys own the ranch next to mine." She shivered. "He looked positively angry."

"I wonder why." Hawkeye closed the tailgate of his truck and placed his hand at the small of Olivia's back. "Not someone you'd want to run into on a dark night."

"No." Olivia started for the staircase leading off the dock to the parking lot.

Before she reached the top step to descend, a voice behind them said, "Miss Dawson."

Olivia stopped and turned toward the man who'd called out her name.

Hawkeye stood partially between them.

"Miss Dawson." He wore khaki slacks and a black windbreaker with LF Enterprises embroidered on the left breast.

"That's me," Olivia said, taking the man's hand.

"Leo Fratiani."

She raised her brows. "Nice to meet you, Mr. Fratiani. Should I know you?"

He smiled. "No, no. I'm new in town. I understand you own the Stone Oak Ranch. Is that right?"

Hawkeye could see the muscles working in Olivia's throat as she swallowed hard before answering.

"Yes, that would be correct," she said, though her voice was strained.

Hawkeye's fingers curled into a fist, ready to take on this man who was causing Olivia pain.

Leo pulled a card from his pocket and handed it to her. "I represent a client interested in purchasing your ranch. Do you have time to talk?"

She dropped the man's hand. Color rose in her cheeks and her lips thinned into a straight line.

Hawkeye almost felt sorry for the man. But not quite. The woman's father wasn't even cold in his grave and already scavengers were feeding on what was left behind.

Fratiani stepped forward. "I only need a few minutes of your time. Then we could set up a better time to go over my client's offer."

Hawkeye stepped between Olivia and the

land agent. "I'm sorry, but Miss Dawson has a prior commitment."

He circled her waist with his arm and led her toward the stairs.

"Would another time be better?" Fratiani called out behind them.

"No," Olivia said through clenched teeth. She descended the stairs and waited while Hawkeye opened the passenger door for her.

With her hand on the door's armrest, she paused before climbing in and glanced up at Hawkeye. "Why does everyone assume I'll sell the ranch? Why can't they just leave me alone?"

Hawkeye pulled her into his arms and held her for a moment. "Don't let him get to you."

"I shouldn't. But I can't help it. It makes me so angry."

"And it should. You have a right to be mad at people like Fratiani coming at you so soon after your father's passing." Hawkeye kissed her temple and would have handed her up into the truck, but a shout went up behind him.

"There he is!"

Hawkeye and Olivia turned toward the sound.

In the short time they'd been inside the store, the crowd had thickened. A limousine pulled up at the edge of the gathering and a man dressed

in a pair of neatly ironed blue jeans and a tai-
lored white button-down dress shirt stepped
out. He'd rolled the sleeves a third of the way
up his arms, giving the appearance of a man
about to go to work on something.

Hawkeye got the impression it was a staged
look and the man was a politician, with his perfectly combed hair and manicured hands, and
his entourage climbing out of the car with him.

Someone held up one of the campaign signs
and started a chant. "We want Morris!"

Olivia muttered a curse word.

Hawkeye glanced her way. "Someone you
know?"

"Grady Morris." She climbed into the truck.
"Let's go."

Hawkeye turned back to the politician, studying him. "You don't want to hear what he has
to say?"

"Not really," Olivia responded.

The man climbed to the porch and waved
at the crowd. "Thank you for coming to my
campaign kickoff. I couldn't start a campaign
without the support of the good people of Grizzly Pass."

Hawkeye walked slowly around the truck,
climbed in and rolled down his window.

"I want you all to know that I will represent the people of Wyoming in Washington. You will not be forgotten."

"What about the Native Americans?" someone shouted.

Morris nodded. "I will do my best to represent the interests of the people who were here first in this great nation."

"How will you help bring jobs back to our state?" another voice questioned loud enough to be heard over the others.

Morris raised his hand as if swearing on a stack of Bibles. "I will work in Washington to help keep our manufacturing jobs from going to foreign countries, and make it more difficult for foreign products to be sold in the States by increasing tariffs on imports."

"And the oil industry?" another man shouted. "What will you do to bring the pipeline back so that we can have our jobs back?"

"No!" a Native American cried. "No to the pipeline crossing our sacred grounds and poisoning our water. Find another way."

"Fine, then how about crossing other grounds?" asked the man who'd asked about bringing the pipeline back. "We need to quit relying on foreign oil and build the infrastructure to get our own oil out of the ground and across the country."

"As your congressman," Morris said, "I promise to address the issues with the oil companies to bring jobs and prosperity back to our state."

"What about reducing the fees for grazing on government land?" a rancher asked.

"I'll work on that, as well." Morris pressed his hand over his heart. "I'll be your voice. Your advocate."

"If you can do all of that, I'll vote for you," someone encouraged.

Another added his approval. "Yeah, me, too."

A woman holding a baby on her hip raised her voice above the others. "How do we know you're not lying? That your promises aren't empty like every other politician's?"

"That's the big question," Olivia muttered. "My father always swore that man was only out for himself. Everything he did was for the almighty dollars that would line his pocket."

"Do you know why your father would have said that? Did he have proof?" Hawkeye asked.

"Morris has always been involved in every deal that could make him money in this state. He's in bed with all of the big corporations and he's willing to do anything it takes to make a profit."

"So he's a businessman. Does that make him untrustworthy?"

"I trusted my father's judgment." Olivia clenched her hands in her lap. "Morris is no better than Fratiani or Bryson Rausch. They want something for nothing. Rausch offered to buy my land, yesterday." Olivia snorted. "He said it would be too hard for a lone woman to run a place as big as Stone Oak Ranch. He'd help me out by taking it off my hands for a quarter of what it's worth."

Hawkeye's lips twitched. He could imagine her reaction to those words. But he held in his smile. "What did you tell him?"

"Hell no." She crossed her arms over her chest. "I didn't appreciate the man's condescending attitude about my ability to run a ranch on my own. I know more about ranching than he knows about good business practices."

Hawkeye released the tension on his lips and allowed his smile to spread across his face. "Good for you." He really liked this woman's spunk.

"I haven't had time to think about *now*, much less my *future*. You'd think people would give me a few days before they descend on me like maggots on roadkill."

Hawkeye cringed. "That's a bit graphic."

She shrugged, her lips twisting into a wry grin. "Yeah, I guess it is, even for me. But Rausch is as low as they come."

"I'll take your word for it." Hawkeye shifted into Drive, but kept his foot on the brake. "Ready to go?"

"More than ready." She cast another glance toward the candidate, her chin tilting upward as they passed Grady Morris. "Just because I'm a woman doesn't disqualify me as a ranch owner. I am my father's daughter. The son he never had."

Hawkeye's lips parted in a smile. "I like that about you. You stand up for yourself and what matters most. You won't let people walk all over you."

"Darn right."

He eased forward, skimming the side of the crowd, careful not to run over anyone. Morris had just concluded his speech and was walking toward his limousine when he caught sight of Olivia in the passenger seat. His gaze followed her the entire time it took for Hawkeye to drive past.

Out of the corner of his view, Hawkeye caught a glimpse of Don Sweeney standing on the loading dock, his narrow-eyed gaze also on Hawkeye's truck. On the porch Morris had just vacated stood Leo Fratiani, leaning against a column, his gaze first on Morris and then switching to Hawkeye's truck.

Interesting. Hawkeye focused on the road ahead. "I'd like to make a stop at the tavern for just a few minutes."

"Are you hungry?" she asked.

"No. I want to meet with Garner and the team."

She glanced his way, her eyes narrowing. "Got anything? Because if you do, I completely missed it."

"Not much. But every clue should be investigated."

Olivia nodded. "Agreed."

Hawkeye drove the three blocks to the tavern and parked at the side close to the stairs up to the loft apartment. Hawkeye dropped down from the vehicle and hurried around to open Olivia's door.

She was already on the ground.

"Do you ever let a man open a door for you?"

She gave him a half smile and shrugged. "I tend to be impatient."

"Noted." Hawkeye waved her by. "After you."

Olivia passed him and climbed the stairs to the apartment.

Garner met them at the door. "Oh, good. I'm glad you came by. What do you have for us?"

"Four names we need you to look into." Hawkeye ushered Olivia into the room. Garner and Hack were the only people present. The other members of the team were nowhere to be seen.

Garner chuckled. "I think we have just about everyone in Grizzly Pass on our list of suspects involved in either murder or plots to overthrow the government or both." Garner sobered. "Seriously, this town isn't that big."

"Check into Don Sweeney," Hawkeye started.

"Wait. Let me get a pen to write with." Garner grabbed a pen from the desk and a pad of paper. "Shoot."

"Do a background check on Don Sweeney, Leo Fratiani, Grady Morris and Bryson Rausch."

Garner's pen stopped midstroke. "Bryson Rausch? As in the pillar of the community, Bryson Rausch? And isn't Grady Morris the man who is running for the US House of Representatives for the state of Wyoming? Have you met them?"

"No." Hawkeye shook his head. "But I saw Morris give his campaign speech in front of the local feed store."

"And something he said set you off?" Garner held up his hand. "Don't get me wrong. I trust your judgment. I'm just curious."

"As a candidate, having upheaval in your state can make you more appealing than the incumbent," Hawkeye said.

Olivia gasped. "Do you think Morris could have killed my father?"

"Right now, I don't know who killed your father." Hawkeye stroked her arm and took her hand in his, squeezing gently. "I'm sure if Morris had killed him, he'd have an ironclad alibi for the day your father died."

"Then why do you want Morris's background checked?" Garner asked.

"He's in a tenuous position. He probably has some ghosts in his closet he doesn't want exposed." Hawkeye turned to Hack. "Can you get into his personal accounts, email, texts, et cetera, and see if anything comes up? I'm not saying he's guilty of anything, but it wouldn't hurt to check him out."

Hack gave Hawkeye a mock salute. "Will do."

"What about Don Sweeney and Leo Fratiani?" Garner asked.

"Sweeney is prior service. A marine with the tattoos to prove it and a boatload of attitude. I'd like to know why he left the military."

"A lot of people leave the military after their enlistment is up," Garner said.

"Yeah, but something tells me Sweeney might not have left voluntarily. He had the Marine Corps emblem tattoo with a skull and crossbones over it. Most marines are proud of their service and wouldn't sully the emblem with anything else."

"Check." Garner nodded. "And Fratiani?"

Hawkeye tipped his head toward Olivia and gave her the opportunity to fill in Garner.

"He hit me up with an offer to purchase my ranch," she said, rubbing her hands over her arms, as if the air in the loft apartment had suddenly chilled. "He wasn't the only one. Rausch offered yesterday. I turned down both of them. My ranch isn't for sale."

Garner's eyes narrowed and they fixed on

Olivia. "You do realize that if your father was murdered, it could be in connection with his ranch. Someone might want it badly enough to kill to own it. If that's the case, you really are in danger."

"I don't care." Her lips thinned. "I'm not selling."

Garner grinned. "I didn't say you should. But you need to be extra careful. You could be the next target."

"All the more reason for me to stay with her at the Stone Oak Ranch." Hawkeye squeezed Olivia's hand. If he had anything to say about it, he'd protect Olivia with his own life. "If someone makes an attempt on Olivia, someone needs to be there to give her some protection and maybe even bring down the perpetrator."

"And if you manage to take him alive, all the better." Garner clapped his hands and rubbed them together. "We really need a live witness to help us pinpoint the kingpin of the Free America movement and put an end to the threat to overthrow the government."

"I'd rather Olivia wasn't a target," Hawkeye said.

Olivia pulled her hand from his and squared her shoulders. "I don't plan on dying anytime soon. You can bet that if someone takes a crack at me, we'll bring him in for investigation."

Garner grinned. "I like your pluck, Miss Dawson."

"Call me Liv," she said.

"Liv it is." Garner smiled. "If you ever need anything, don't hesitate to ask."

"Thank you," Olivia said.

If Hawkeye wasn't mistaken, the ranch owner's eyes filled with tears, and she'd probably rather die than let them fall.

Blinking them back, she squared her shoulders again. "Now, if we're done here, we have a lot of work to do before sundown."

"We'll get to work on those names." Garner clapped a hand on Hawkeye's shoulder. "Be sure to yell if you need backup."

"You bet I will," Hawkeye promised. He'd seen how quickly events could escalate by the two incidents that had already occurred in the Grizzly Pass area. The kidnapping of a busload of children had happened so quickly, no one had anticipated the horror. It had taken their entire team and additional help from the sheriff's department and Homeland Security to get that disaster under control.

And the team had been mobilized again to

bring one of their members out of a hunt where he and a local female had been the targets.

Damn right he'd call for backup if he smelled even a hint of trouble.

He prayed that Olivia's misfortune wouldn't continue. But he wouldn't place bets on peace and tranquillity. Not now. Not until they found the man responsible and fully understood his motivation for killing her father.

Chapter Eight

Liv settled back in her seat, her mind moving a hundred times faster than the speed of the truck. "When I came back to Grizzly Pass, I thought my father had died due to an accident. That was hard enough to accept. But now…" She shook her head. "If someone killed him for his land…" Her fists clenched in her lap and she ground her teeth together. The injustice burned like a fire in her belly.

"We don't know that for sure yet."

"But you and Garner seem to think it has something to do with the ranch and maybe even the man you were chasing yesterday. Didn't you say he was trying to blow up the pipeline?"

"It appeared to be his goal."

"And he crossed onto my property to escape, as if he'd been across my land before and knew his way. It's easy to get lost in the hills. He had to know how to get back to the road across that corner of the ranch."

Hawkeye nodded. "That would be my assumption. I had a contour map to get around with, and it was slow going because I didn't know the existing trails and paths. The man I chased out of the hills knew the way."

"Through my property." Olivia clamped her teeth together, anger simmering. What was important enough to kill a man who'd done nothing to anyone? A man who'd spent his life working with his land and livestock? Again, her heart pinched in her chest. If she found out who'd done this, she'd…she'd…

Hell, she wanted to kill the one responsible. But if she did, would she be any better than him? Would her father want her to risk going to jail for killing a man who'd taken his life?

Still the anger roiled.

By the time they'd entered the gate to Stone Oak Ranch, Liv was ready to jump out of the truck and run all the way up the driveway to the barn. Her pent-up rage and energy were ready to explode into action. Holding them back challenged her patience like nothing before. But she did hold them back. All the way to the barn, where Hawkeye pulled his truck to a stop.

She was out of the truck and lowering the tailgate before Hawkeye had time to shift into Park and turn off the engine.

CJ emerged from the barn, sweat-soaked and pushing a full wheelbarrow of straw and horse dung. He parked the wheelbarrow to the side and hurried over to grab a sack of feed. The teen didn't look strong enough to carry the fifty-pound bag, but he slung it over his shoulder like a pro and carried it into the barn without being asked or told to help.

Liv smiled across the bed of the truck at Hawkeye. "I like him already."

Hawkeye nodded. "Me, too." He gathered two bags, lifting them to his shoulder.

Liv loaded a feed bag onto her own shoulder and followed the ranger into the barn, admiring his strength and stamina. She could sure use someone like him on the ranch.

As soon as the thought emerged, she squashed it. The man was all about his military connection. He'd want to return to his unit as soon as his assignment was up in Grizzly Pass.

Liv couldn't get used to having him around. She'd really have to get onto the task of hiring a ranch hand soon. Abe wouldn't be able to help for weeks and CJ's school would be back in session soon, leaving her to handle everything by herself.

She wanted to keep the ranch, but she knew her limitations. It took her father and Abe working full-time and then some to keep up. And they hired additional ranch hands at roundup to work the ranch, tag, vaccinate, deworm and castrate the young steers. It was a huge effort, requiring veterinary, management and accounting skills to run a place like Stone Oak Ranch. Liv couldn't do it on her own. But maybe if she had at least one really good ranch hand, Abe could manage the books while he recuperated.

Once the feed bags were stacked and two had been poured into bins, Liv inspected CJ's work in the stalls. He'd done as good a job, if not a better one, mucking stalls as Liv would have. "Great work, CJ."

The teen's cheeks turned a ruddy red. "Thank you, ma'am."

"Call me Liv. *Ma'am* makes me feel old," she said with a smile.

"Yes, ma'am— Sorry, Miss Liv." Again the blush rose in his cheeks.

Liv flattened her smile, not wanting to embarrass the youth any more than she already had.

"I had planned on cleaning the horses' hooves and exercising them this afternoon," CJ said. "Unless there's something else you'd like me to work on."

"No. That will be perfect." Liv studied the teen. "You have cared for horses' hooves before?"

His eyes widened. "Oh, yes, ma'am—er— Miss Liv. My stepfather has four horses at home. I usually take care of them. I learned from the farrier how to do it when I was eight. I've been doing it ever since."

Eight? Liv was amazed at this young man who seemed older than his sixteen years. "Just be careful not to dig too deep."

The teen nodded. "I'll be very careful. I love to work with horses and they seem to like me."

"I'll be out this afternoon checking fences with Mr. Walsh. If you need anything, I won't be much help. If you get into any trouble, call the sheriff. It's near lunchtime now. You're welcome to make yourself at home in the kitchen. There's peanut butter and jelly and a loaf of bread."

"Thank you, Miss Liv." He ducked his head. "I really appreciate the job."

She couldn't help herself. Liv leaned close and hugged the teen's bony shoulders. "And I appreciate the help."

"What time do you expect to be back?" CJ asked.

"Before the sun sets," she answered. "But if we're not back by then, don't worry. We'll be okay."

"I have to be home an hour before dark to take care of my chores. Do you want me to stay until you get back?"

"No, but there is something you can do this afternoon before you leave." Liv tipped her head. "Follow me," she called over her shoulder. "You can come too, Mr. Walsh."

CJ and Hawkeye followed her to a separate garage behind the house. Inside was a collection of dusty antique furniture, car parts and tool chests. In the far corner was something under a faded and dusty tarp.

Liv suppressed her smile as she pulled the tarp off, sending a cloud of dust flying into the air.

When the cloud cleared, she could see her old scooter. "I used this scooter through college in Seattle. It got me around great, although I don't recommend driving it in the snow and ice."

CJ shook his head and looked from the scooter to Liv. "I don't understand. Do you want me to fix it for you? Fix it to sell?"

"It should be in good working condition. My father was pretty consistent about cranking it up at least once or twice a year. He'd change the oil, even if he didn't use it." She inhaled and let out the breath in a long steady stream. "It's yours if you want it."

CJ's eyes widened and he shook his head. "I can't accept it."

"Of course you can. I want an employee who can get here on time every day. Again, I don't expect you to drive it on icy roads. In fact, I don't want you to drive it in the winter at all." She touched his arm. "Promise you won't drive it on icy roads. I'd never be able to live with myself if something happened to you on this contraption."

CJ continued to shake his head. "I can't accept it."

"Why not? It's either that or it goes back under the tarp and deteriorates until it's no longer any good for anyone."

Despite her efforts to convince him, Liv couldn't get him to quit shaking his head.

"If I take this home, my stepfather will claim

it as his. He says that anything he finds on his property is his."

"Then park it just off his property and walk in."

The teen's face brightened and then he chewed on his lip. "I suppose I could hide it in the woods by the road. Ernie doesn't have to know."

Liv didn't like setting the kid up to lie to his stepfather, but Ernie was just mean enough to take CJ's only method of transportation, forcing the teen to use his rusty bicycle or walk the ten miles to Stone Oak Ranch.

CJ walked forward and ran his hand across the vinyl seat. "Why are you doing this for me?" he whispered.

"I'm not doing it so much for you as for me," Liv said. "I need to know you won't have problems getting here, and I need to know you won't be too tired to work."

The teen shot a glance back at Liv. "May I sit on it?"

"You bet. I hope you can get it going before you leave."

CJ swung his leg over the seat and sat on the smooth faux leather. "I'll work on it after I take care of the horses."

"Good. Try not to do anything that will cause you injury, since no one will be here as your backup."

"I'm used to working on my own," CJ said. "And you don't have to pay me at all. I'll work off the cost of the scooter. I could never repay you for your generosity." He twisted the throttle handle.

"Repaying me isn't necessary, and I intend to pay you for your work. But you'll have to get your mother's permission to ride the scooter."

"She'll let me."

"And your stepfather?"

"What he doesn't know won't hurt me." The teen's face hardened. "As long as I have my mother's permission, it shouldn't be a problem."

"Thank you for helping out. With my foreman in the hospital, I wasn't sure how I would manage." Liv smiled. "Now I have to get to work mending fences."

"I could help with the fences," CJ said, his tone eager, his enthusiasm contagious. "I know how to stretch wire and I'm pretty handy with a hammer."

"I really need you to take care of the animals around here. I'm sure I'll take you up on that offer another time." Liv cast a glance toward Hawkeye. "Ready?"

"You bet." He followed her out into the open. "You made that kid's day."

"I just hope I don't cause more problems between him and his stepfather."

"I'm sure that comes with the territory for CJ. I don't think there's much love lost between Ernie and the kid." Hawkeye glanced around. "We're taking my truck?"

She shook her head and walked toward the pasture. "No. The trails are too narrow for a full-size truck to make it safely onto the back end of the property in the hills." She stood at the gate to the pasture and gave a shrill whistle.

Her gray gelding trotted up to the fence and nuzzled her hand. "I'm taking Stormy. You can choose any horse you might like to ride. They're all trained for ranch work and are familiar with trail riding."

HAWKEYE SHOOK HIS HEAD. As tempted as he was, a promise was a promise. "I'll pass."

"You're missing out. Riding horses up into the hills is much more serene than taking loud, motorized vehicles." Liv caught Stormy's bridle and snapped a lead onto one of the metal rings. She turned to Hawkeye. "There are two four-wheelers in the back of the barn. You're welcome to take one of them. You can carry the barbed wire and fence staples."

Hawkeye reached out to rub the gelding's nose. "Thank you for understanding."

Liv led the horse toward the barn. "I understand, but I'm sure your mother wouldn't hold you to a promise you made when you were a kid. Especially since you've been to war and faced much worse circumstances than being tossed from a horse."

He nodded. "True. And someday, I might change my mind, but for now, I'd rather not ride a horse."

"I respect that, but you'll have to stay back a ways so that you don't spook my horse on some of the more difficult trails."

"Are you sure you don't want to ride a four-wheeler?" Hawkeye suggested. "You said you had two."

"I prefer horseback." She led her horse into the barn and tied him to a post. "I only take the motorized vehicles when I have to carry fence posts or other large items that would be too bulky on horseback."

"Like rolls of barbed wire?"

She nodded, her lips turning up slightly at the corners. As he suspected, she'd planned on him taking the four-wheeler all along. If he didn't have to carry the barbed wire and staples, he'd be tempted to break his promise and ride a horse, just to prove to her that he wasn't afraid. But not today. They had real work to do and would need the tools and supplies to accomplish the job.

"Fair enough," he said. "While you saddle up, I'll check the status of my transportation."

Grabbing the roll of barbed wire and the bucket of staples, Hawkeye walked to the back of the barn and found two four-wheelers tucked beneath the ladder leading up to the loft. Neither vehicle was new, and both had been scuffed enough to indicate they'd been used on rough terrain. Each ATV had metal mesh racks on the front and back and a rifle scabbard mounted on the right side.

Hawkeye dropped the bucket of fence staples and the roll of barbed wire in the back rack and secured them with bungee cords and metal ties. He found a couple of hammers in the tack room and a come-along hanging on the wall.

As part of his upbringing on the ranch, he'd learned many skills, including proper fence building and mending. He'd need to bring every tool necessary with him or the project would end before it started. Once they were up in the mountains, it wouldn't be so easy to run back to the barn for supplies or equipment.

Once he had everything loaded and tied down, he shifted the ATV to Neutral and pushed it out the back door of the barn before twisting the key in the ignition.

The engine leaped to life, blowing very little smoke. Olivia's father and foreman had kept the ATVs in good working order.

Hawkeye mounted and revved the accelerator while still in Neutral before shifting it into gear and driving it around to the front of the barn.

Olivia stood with the saddled gray, the reins draped over her gloved hands. "I'll get the gate." She led the horse to the fence, pulled back the bar and let the gate swing open.

Hawkeye drove past her and waited on the other side of the fence for Olivia to lead her horse through, close the gate and mount. She took off at a trot across the pasture and up into the hills, following a broad trail that was wide enough for his truck. That trail started to narrow to barely the width of the four-wheeler's tires.

Hawkeye trailed fifty feet behind, careful not to get too close and spook Stormy. He lost sight of Olivia at several sharp bends in the path, but would soon spot her ahead. Every time she slipped from his view, his heart pounded and he instinctively goosed the accelerator, kicking up gravel and rocks beneath his tires. He could see the benefit of riding a horse in that the only sound would be the clip-clop of the animal's hooves on the stones.

The roar of the ATV engine drowned out all other sounds around Hawkeye, a fact he regretted. If Olivia were to scream, he probably wouldn't hear it until it was too late. If she'd driven another four-wheeler, at least he could have followed her more closely, keeping her within his line of sight at all times.

Surely the promise he'd made to his mother had reached its statute of limitations. Given the severity of the situation on Stone Oak Ranch, Hawkeye needed every advantage he could get. Hearing the enemy before he saw them would be a major advantage. One he currently couldn't claim. He found himself more than a little frustrated the entire journey to the far northwestern corner of the ranch.

Rounding yet another outcropping of rock,

he searched for the woman on horseback and held his breath until he found her. She'd stopped near a fence post where the wire had been cut and the barbed strands lay in big coils several feet away.

Olivia sat on her horse, staring down at the fence. Then she swung her leg over the side and dropped down out of the saddle to the hard, rocky ground. For a long moment, she stared at the rocks, not the destroyed fence. Sunlight glinted off giant tears welling up in her eyes.

Hawkeye pulled his four-wheeler to a stop on the edge of the clearing, shut off the engine and climbed off. "What's wrong?"

Olivia continued to stare at the ground. "This is where he died." Then she looked up, the evidence of her grief clearly written across her face. Big tears slipped over the lower edges of her eyelids, ran down to her chin and dropped into the dirt. She sniffed and wiped at her tears. "I'm sorry. I'm not normally so weepy."

He crossed to her and pulled her into his arms, resting her cheek on his chest. "You have every right to be weepy."

"But it accomplishes nothing. My dad would have told me it's a waste of time and energy." She laughed, choking on a sob. "I never pointed out to him that he'd cried when my mother died. He didn't know I saw him by the barn, bent double, sobbing. My dad cried, too. That made him even more human and caring." She stared up at Hawkeye, tears trembling in her lashes. "I loved him so much."

Hawkeye gathered her closer and kissed her forehead. "I would like to have met him."

"Thanks for putting up with me."

"I wouldn't call it putting up with you. I kind of like holding you." He smoothed the hair back from her forehead and pressed a kiss there.

Liv leaned into him, her fingers curling into his chest. She held on, prolonging the pressure of his lips on her skin.

He loved the way she felt against him and the way she smelled of the outdoors. But holding her wasn't getting the work done.

She must have come to the same conclusion because she straightened and pushed away from him. "Come on. We have a fence to mend before dark."

"Before we start on the fence, I'd like to cross over onto the other side and explore."

"I could start laying out the barbed wire and tools, while you do your thing on the other side," Olivia offered. "Then, when you get back, I'll show you how quickly I can string wire."

Before she finished speaking, Hawkeye was shaking his head. "You heard Garner. If someone wants this ranch bad enough to hurt your father, you're as much of a target."

She pulled a handgun from beneath her jacket and waved it in the air. "I can protect myself."

Hawkeye touched his finger to the barrel and pushed it away. "I'm sure you can handle yourself, but I'd feel better if you stayed right with me. I didn't even like it when you rode ahead of me on your horse."

She gave him a sassy glance from beneath her lashes. "Maybe next time, you'll ride a horse and we can stay closer."

"Or you can ride the other four-wheeler." He touched a finger to her cheek. "Please. Come with me for a few minutes. I'd like to see if I missed anything when I was chasing Demolition Man yesterday."

"All right. But I doubt anyone would want to hurt me. I haven't stayed here in years." She started for her horse, but Hawkeye grabbed her arm and pulled her short.

"Ride with me," he said, keeping the request low, insistent, a warm entreaty in her ear.

He prayed she couldn't resist the request when he made it seem so personal.

Her eyes flared wider, and her gaze dropped to his lips. She sighed. "Fine. I'll go with you."

"On the back of my four-wheeler," he said.

"I'd rather ride my horse."

"It puts too much distance between the two of us. I don't feel comfortable going off your property into government-controlled land where anyone could be watching or waiting."

"Anyone could be watching and waiting on my property." She swept her hand toward the downed fence.

"You have a point." He tipped his head toward the four-wheeler and gave her his best bone-melting half smile. "You can drive, if you want."

LIV'S HEART FLUTTERED and butterflies erupted in her belly. How could one man have such a hold over her? When he put it that way, with that smile... *Damn.* Who was she kidding? Though she wasn't eager to be in close proximity to the man who made her blood sing every time he got too close, she couldn't resist. But if they were going to ride double on a four-wheeler, she preferred to do the driving. It might be the only thing she had control over. She sure as heck didn't have control over her reactions to the man.

Liv climbed onto the ATV and waited for Hawkeye to get on the back.

When he did, he wrapped his arms around her waist and leaned his body into hers.

Holy hell, she was entirely too aware of the man holding on to her. Perhaps she'd have been better off riding on the back of the ATV. At least then she could have held on to the ATV seat, instead of wrapping her arms around Hawkeye's waist.

She'd let him drive back. At least then she wouldn't have his arms around her waist and she wouldn't be so confused…and…turned on.

Chapter Nine

Hawkeye held on tightly around Olivia's waist. Not only because he liked being close to her, but because she drove like a bat out of hell. If he hadn't held on, she'd have lost him a couple of times going around some of the tighter corners along the trail.

Thankfully, she seemed to know her way. He recognized the shapes of the ridges and the rugged trails down into the gorges. As they neared the trail down into the valley where he'd found the man planting the dynamite near the pipeline, he yelled, "Slow down."

Olivia brought the ATV to a halt on the top of the ridge overlooking the area.

Hawkeye cast a glance around, taking in the other hilltops, searching for any movement. Anyone with a weapon perched on the ridgelines could easily pick off someone at the bottom. His military training made him look at terrain that way. He was glad of that training. Not only had someone tried to plant explosives at this pipeline checkpoint, but a pipeline inspector had been killed there. Shot from one of the surrounding ridges.

Yeah, Hawkeye would do well to treat this as enemy territory and be prepared for anything. "Let's go to the bottom. I want to check on something."

"Is this the place?" Olivia asked.

His chest tightened and he gave the neighboring hills another once-over with a trained eye. "Yeah."

Olivia thumbed the throttle lever and eased the four-wheeler down the trail into the valley.

Hawkeye had her park it in the shadows of a lodgepole pine tree. When he got off, he pointed to the tree's trunk. "Stay here. If there is anyone after you, you won't present a decent target hidden in the shadows."

Olivia shook her head. "I'm not hiding from anyone. I have just as much right to be here as anyone else." She started past him.

Hawkeye snagged her arm and pulled her against his chest. "You aren't wearing a bullet-proof vest or a Kevlar helmet. If someone takes a shot at you, you're dead. Who will take care of your family's ranch?"

"If I die, who cares? I don't have any family to leave the ranch to." Her lips pressed into a thin line, her shoulders pushing back, displaying an inner strength and a willingness to charge into danger and seek justice. But the mist in Olivia's eyes reminded Hawkeye of just how vulnerable she still was, having lost her father—the only relative she'd had left in the world.

"Yeah, you might not have a family to leave the ranch to, but you have an employee who, if I'm guessing right, is just as much a part of the family as your father. If you die, the ranch will be sold to the highest bidder and Abe will be out of a job. At his age, and still recovering from his broken leg, he'll have difficulty finding work."

Olivia frowned at Hawkeye. "Yeah, hit me where it hurts. Okay, I'll stay close to the shadows and I won't stand in one place very long. How's that? Make you more comfortable being with the walking target?" She gave him a wink, shook off his hand on her arm, strode out into the open and glanced at the disturbed ground where the dynamite had been planted and retrieved.

Hawkeye followed her, staying close, offering his body up as her first line of defense against gunfire.

"Seriously?" She pushed him away. "I don't want you taking a bullet for me. But thanks for the thought." After a quick inspection of the vicinity around the site, she stepped back into the shadows.

Hawkeye's lips quirked at the corners. He made a wider sweep of the area, looking for anything his dynamite-planting bad guy might have dropped. The place was clean.

"Anything else you want to look at while we're on this side of the fence?" Olivia asked, her gaze on the surrounding hills. "The sun drops behind the mountains a good thirty minutes before the scheduled sundown for this area. And from the looks of it, we'll have a cloudy night, which means darkness will come even sooner."

He glanced up at the surrounding hills. "Do you know of any caves around here?"

She nodded. "My dad and I used to explore the caves in the mountains whenever he had time. There are some with cave paintings hundreds of years old."

"Far from here?"

"Not very." She looked around. "It's been years, but I think I can find them. We'd better hurry, or we won't have time to mend the fence and get back to the house before dark."

Hawkeye glanced up at the thick gray clouds rolling in above the ridges. "We'll give it thirty minutes. If we don't find the caves by then, we'll head back."

Olivia nodded. "Deal." She climbed onto the four-wheeler and scooted forward.

Hawkeye hid a grin. He liked that Olivia was no-nonsense and brave. But he also worried she wasn't taking the threat to her life as seriously as he was. Her father was dead. You couldn't undo that. And the woman was growing on him. He'd hate to lose her when he was just getting to know her.

He slipped onto the back of the ATV, wrapped his arms around her narrow waist and inhaled the mix of herbal shampoo and the outdoors. Both scents would forever remind him of Olivia, even when he was back in some hellishly hot desert in the Middle East.

The thought of returning to war sobered him.

Being on a ranch had brought back the good memories with the bad. Yeah, he'd lost his little sister, but working with the horses and cattle had always made him feel like his efforts counted. He could see the results of his efforts. Not so much in the army.

As for the horses, it wasn't that he didn't like them. He loved them. And he liked the smell of freshly cut hay and the earthy aroma of manure. Hell, he'd shoveled his share growing up. He could almost feel the straining muscles and the sweat of a hot summer's day working in the hay fields of Texas.

Hawkeye shook himself free of his memories and focused on the hills around him. By letting Olivia drive, he maintained the freedom to study the bluffs, searching for easily accessible caves.

When the day-care children had been kidnapped and trapped in an abandoned mine, their caregivers had discovered empty crates and boxes that had stored a pretty impressive number of AR-15 rifles. Which led them to ask: Who'd had the money to purchase so many? And even more disturbing was the question of where all the semiautomatic rifles had disappeared to.

These hills were riddled with natural caves and abandoned mines from the gold-rush era of the 1800s. There were any number of places someone could have hidden the rifles.

Hell, they could be in someone's barn or in a basement. Unless they discovered a list of the names of all the Free America members, they didn't really have a place to start looking or a chance at a warrant to search premises. So far, they only had a few names of suspected members. A judge wouldn't give a warrant to search based on pure supposition.

But something about this place out in the mountains meant something to someone. Enough for people to be murdered—the pipeline inspector and potentially Olivia's father. And it appeared that someone wanted the valley to be destroyed via dynamite.

Why? What was so important in these hills that people were dying over it?

Olivia shouted over the roar of the engine. "Check it out!" She pointed to the hillside ahead of her.

When the trail would have wound around a bluff to the right, she slowed to a stop and shut down the engine so they could talk.

"That's one of the caves my father and I explored. I remember because it had a huge boulder in front of it that was shaped like a sitting frog." She smiled sadly. "The last time I was here, I was only fourteen. My dad and I rode horses out here and camped under the stars."

She started the engine and rounded the bend in the trail, curving along the side of the hill until they descended to a grassy glen at the foot of the cave entrance.

Hawkeye hopped off the ATV and held out his hand.

Olivia took it and swung her leg over the seat, dropping to the ground. She smiled. "There's the ring of stones my father put together for a fire." She walked across to the charred stones and frowned. Dropping to her haunches, she pushed aside the charred remains of a log and held her hand over a bed of ashes. "These are a lot more recent than anything from the last time I was here. Based on the residual warmth of the embers beneath the log, I'd say they were from last night." She straightened and glanced around.

Hawkeye stood close, turning his back to her, facing outward to the nearby hills. He didn't like that there were so many vantage points above them. A sniper would have an easy target to aim for. "Let's check out that cave," he said, backing toward her.

Olivia climbed the gravel-and-boulder-strewn incline to the cave's entrance. She pulled her pistol from where it was tucked into her waistband and disappeared into the shadows.

His pulse quickening, Hawkeye hurried in after her, his weapon drawn. It took a moment for his eyesight to adjust to the darkness. When it did, he was amazed at how big the inside of the cave was compared to the narrow entry. The trickle of light was just enough to illuminate the walls closest to the entrance.

"Look." Olivia stood near the side of the cave, staring at the wall in front of her.

Hawkeye studied the interior of the cavern, searching for any movement. The dark abyss of a tunnel gaped like an open maw. Without a flashlight, he didn't have a chance of penetrating its inky depths.

In the limited lighting, he could make out the cave wall and rudimentary drawings in dark red, mustard yellow and black. One was a picture of a bear standing tall in front of a hunter holding a spear. Another painting included two figures sporting clubs in a face-off with what appeared to be a pack of wolves.

"Aren't these beautiful?" Olivia whispered, as if they stood in a library or a museum.

"Incredible." Hawkeye sighed. "I wish I'd thought to bring a flashlight."

"Like this?" A click echoed off the cave walls and a narrow beam of light cut a line through the darkness. Olivia held a small key chain flashlight in her hand. "It's not much, but I carry it in my pocket in case I need it in a pinch."

As he took the light from Olivia's hand, Hawkeye shook his head, leaned in and captured her lips in a quick kiss. "You are an amazing woman."

Hawkeye shone the light around the interior of the cave. The beam didn't go far, but it was far enough to see that the cave wasn't that deep and nothing but the paintings were of interest inside. He returned the beam to its original position and caught Olivia with her fingers touching her lips.

Her cheeks were pink and her eyes narrowed slightly. "You really shouldn't kiss me."

He liked that he'd flustered her. "Why not?"

"Because it makes me want to kiss you back..." she said, her voice trailing off, her eyes widening as he closed the distance between them.

"Does it?" Hawkeye wrapped his arm around her waist and drew her body against his. "Then I should kiss you again." He didn't know why he was pushing the issue, but he knew he couldn't resist another kiss from this strong, beautiful woman. He lowered his head, his lips hovering over hers. "Show me."

LIV'S HEART FLUTTERED and a deep ache built inside her belly, spreading lower. She leaned up on her toes and pressed her mouth to his.

As soon as they connected, Hawkeye's arm tightened around her, crushing her against him. His tongue drew a line along the seam of her lips.

She opened to him and met his tongue stroke for stroke, loving the taste and feel of him. Until she kissed Hawkeye, Liv had never known a desire so intense that she forgot everything around her.

When her lungs reminded her she needed air, she tore her mouth from his and sucked in ragged, shaky breaths. "What is wrong with me?"

Hawkeye leaned his cheek against her temple. "Nothing. As far as I can tell, you're just about perfect."

She shook her head. "The more I learn about what's been happening around here, the more I'm convinced my father was murdered. And I'm standing in a cave kissing a stranger when I should be out searching for my father's killer." She stared up at him. "I must be a very bad person."

"Or a very good kisser." He brushed a light kiss over her mouth. "But you're right. We should be focusing on what's going on. There will be time for kisses later."

If you're still around. Liv didn't say the words out loud, but she felt them, and it added more sadness to her heart, already breaking over the loss of her father.

As if on cue, they broke apart.

Liv turned toward the back of the cave. "Is there nothing in here of interest?"

"Nothing but the paintings and us." He rested his fingers in the small of her back and led her to the cave entrance. Then he took her hand as they walked and slid down the slippery slope to where they'd parked the four-wheeler in the shade of a bush.

Liv liked the feel of his big hand holding

hers. She'd never thought of herself as a girlie-girl, but Hawkeye made her feel delicate and protected. Her chest swelled at his touch, and for a moment she felt some things were right in a world gone wrong.

With her hand on the ATV's grip, Liv was about to throw her leg over the seat when Hawkeye touched her arm. "Do you hear that?"

She was so caught up in her blossoming feelings for the army ranger, Liv hadn't noticed the buzz of small engines until five ATVs popped up over the top of a ridge and came careening down the hillside straight for where she and Hawkeye were standing. Each of the riders wore a dark helmet and dark clothing, and they didn't appear to be slowing down a bit as they barreled down the side of the hill.

"What the hell?" Liv said.

"Damn, they've got guns," Hawkeye said.

At the same time Hawkeye made note of that fact, Liv saw one of the men aiming a handgun at them. A shot rang out, echoing against the bluffs. Dirt kicked up at Liv's feet, making her jump back.

"Let's get out of here!" Hawkeye jumped on the bike, started the engine and barely waited long enough for Liv to hop on the back and wrap her arms around his middle.

He thumbed the throttle, sending the four-wheeler leaping forward, heading for the trail that had brought them down into the valley.

Liv craned her neck, staring back at the five ATVs rushing toward them. She held on tighter and screamed, "Faster!"

Hawkeye bumped up onto the trail and gunned the accelerator, spinning loose rocks and gravel up in their wake.

The five pursuers didn't slow. They hit the grassy glen and sped up, rocketing across the flat expanse and up onto the trail Liv and Hawkeye were following. It wouldn't be long before they caught up.

They had to find a place to hide or set up a defensive position. Hell, Liv wasn't the army guy—Hawkeye was. Surely he had a plan.

They rounded a bend in the trail heading back toward her ranch. At the rate the others were racing along, they'd catch up before Liv and Hawkeye made it to the fence. Not that the broken strands of barbed wire would stop the gang. Continuing to run wasn't an option.

The trail curved around a jutting bluff, blocking her view of their pursuers, which meant they couldn't see her and Hawkeye, either. If only they could throw them off.

Think, Liv. Think!

Then she remembered a maze of huge boulders and a line of caves carved out of the rocky hillside in the valley on the other side of the upcoming ridge.

The trail would split ahead. The left fork would take them back to her property.

As they neared the fork in the trail, Liv yelled over the sound of the engine, "Take the right fork."

Already halfway turned toward the left, Hawkeye yanked the handlebar to the right, making them skid sideways. He held on tightly to keep the ATV from tumbling over the edge of the trail and down a steep hill into a stand of trees.

Liv glanced behind them. The dust cloud that plumed behind them was caught in the breeze and blown toward the left fork. If they could round the next bend in the next two seconds, they might succeed in throwing off the gang of bikers behind them.

She held her breath, turned halfway in her seat and watched for the following vehicles to emerge from behind the bluff outcropping.

Hawkeye spun the four-wheeler around a bend in the trail and still Liv hadn't seen the trailing vehicles. "When you get to the huge boulder at the base of the hill, swing around behind it!" she yelled into Hawkeye's ear.

He nodded without slowing, hurtling around the curves descending into another narrow valley between hilltops.

Liv watched behind them, her heart pounding each time she thought she caught a glimpse of the others behind them. If they could make the boulder-strewn valley before the others, they could lose them in the maze of bus-size boulders and very rough terrain.

At the bottom of the trail, Hawkeye slowed and swung around the back side of the giant boulder Liv remembered from when she was a teen. The ground was littered with larger rocks, making the going a lot more difficult and much slower. But the rocks wouldn't leave tracks. If they could stay hidden from above, they had a chance at making it to one of the caves where they could hide.

Liv held on for dear life, nearly tossed several times as they rumbled across the rocks and clung to the lengthening shadows of the hillside. Soon the sun was completely hidden behind a dark gray pall of clouds and darkness descended on the rocky valley.

When she thought they might have escaped the others, Liv tugged on Hawkeye's arm and pointed to one of the caves hidden behind a huge rocky outcropping. "There."

He aimed the four-wheeler toward the cave and drove up the steep slope through the entrance and cut the engine as soon as they were inside.

Liv and Hawkeye jumped off and pushed the vehicle the rest of the way inside, hiding it in the darkness.

Pulling her mini flashlight from her pocket, Liv shone it into the interior of the cave, praying they hadn't walked into the den of a wolf or a bear. Or worse, that they'd stumbled into a timber rattler's home.

She shivered in the damp coolness of the cavern, clicked off the light when she was certain they were safe from what was inside the space. Then she crept up to the edge of the entrance and stood beside Hawkeye.

"I can still hear their engines," he whispered.

She listened, her heartbeat fluttering. "Me, too. But it's getting dark. I'll bet they're not willing to keep looking when the sun is setting. It's too easy to get lost in the mountains."

Hawkeye snorted. "Tell me about it." He glanced down at her. "I'm going out to perform a little recon to see how close they are."

"I'll go with you," she said.

"No. Two people are easier to spot than one."

"And if you get into trouble?" She raised her brows. "Who has your six?"

"I'll stay out of sight."

"So will I."

"Anyone ever tell you that you're stubborn?"

She nodded. "Many times. I consider it one of my good traits."

He shook his head. "Fine. But if I say get down, do it, immediately."

She gave him a mock salute and followed him out of the cave.

They crept along the base of the rocky bluff stretching the length of the narrow valley until they came close to the stand of boulders blocking their view of the trail.

Liv could hear the rumble of engines close by. Too close.

She laid her hand on Hawkeye's arm. "Let's go back."

He touched a finger across her lips. "Stay here," he whispered. "I want to see if I recognize any of them."

"And get yourself killed?" Liv increased the pressure on his arm. "Don't."

"I'll be okay." He gripped her arms. "But only if you stay put. If you come after me, I'll lose focus and we might both be found." He pressed a firm kiss on her lips. "Promise me you'll stay."

Liv wanted to tell him no. She couldn't promise not to follow him. But the intensity of his gaze made her nod. "Okay. I promise."

"Good girl." He kissed her again. "I'll be right back." Then he slipped away into the shadows of dusk.

Before long, Liv couldn't pick him out from among the boulders. She hunkered down in case someone was watching from above and remained as still as she could, straining to hear what was going on.

The engines had been shut off. Male voices bounced off the sides of the bluffs, their echoes making them sound like they were closer than they were.

Liv held her breath, waiting for a shout to go up that they'd found Hawkeye. If that happened, all bets were off and she'd come out fighting. She had her pistol. She had at least ten rounds in the magazine.

With her hand on the weapon, she waited, counting to one hundred, then counting to one hundred again. By the time she'd counted backward from one hundred, she had waited as long as she possibly could. Liv bunched her muscles and started to rise.

One of the men's shouts was loud and clear. "Let's go!"

Engines fired to life and took off, heading back the way they'd come. Did they have Hawkeye with them? Was he lying on the ground, bleeding out? Had they crushed his skull?

Scenario after horrible scenario ran through Liv's head. She was on her feet and had taken two steps in the direction Hawkeye had disappeared when he emerged from the shadows and pulled her into his arms.

"Why are you shaking?" he asked, rubbing his hands up and down her back.

"Damn you," she said into his shirt. "You had me so worried." She hadn't realized she was shaking until he'd called attention to the fact. Her teeth were chattering and she was cold.

"We need to get you out of here and back home."

"We can't leave. What if that gang is waiting at the fork in the road, or if they've gone to where the fence is down and are lying in wait to jump out and cut us down?"

Hawkeye sighed. "You're right. But it's too cold to stand out here. Let's go back to the four-wheeler. If the stars and the moon come out tonight, we might be able to find our way home."

Liv nodded, not really ready to step out of Hawkeye's embrace to walk back across the increasingly difficult, ankle-twisting terrain.

The clouds descended on the mountains, cutting off any light from the stars above, making it harder and harder to see. They almost missed the cave, finally finding it when they were nearly past the hidden entrance.

Stumbling inside, Liv stood with her arms wrapped around her middle. "Now what?"

"I'm going to find some firewood."

"We can't light a fire. What if they see us?"

"For later. They won't stay out in the cold if they don't have to. Besides, as well hidden as this cave is, they won't see the glow of the flames."

A fire sounded good. The later it got, the more the air temperature dropped.

"I hope they don't find Stormy," Liv said, through chattering teeth.

"I'm betting your horse is back at the barn by now."

Liv smiled. When Stormy was hungry, there wasn't much that could stop him on his way back to the barn for feed. Her biggest worries for the night were the return of the trigger-happy four-wheeler terrorists and the chilled air.

If they didn't start a fire, they could die of exposure. It wasn't unusual for the temperatures in the late summer to be in the high eighties during the day and drop into the low fifties, even forties, at night. She'd even seen it snow in the mountains in August.

"I'll help with the firewood," Liv said and walked outside with Hawkeye.

Fortunately, some was close by and they didn't have to go far to gather enough logs and kindling for a decent blaze.

By the time they returned to the cave, what little lingering daylight that had helped them find the cave in the first place had been leached from the sky and replaced by inky blackness.

Liv touched the button for the mini flashlight, which gave them just enough light to arrange some stones in a circle and place the kindling and firewood in the center.

"I don't suppose you have a match or a lighter?" Hawkeye asked.

Liv shone the light toward the four-wheeler. "We used to keep a small survival kit in the storage compartment of each four-wheeler, and in our saddlebags in case we got caught out at night. I can't imagine my dad changing things up." She handed the flashlight to him and rummaged in the small compartment, unearthing a box of matches. She kissed the box. "Thanks, Dad." Then she handed them to Hawkeye and watched as he used only one match and coaxed the tinder into a flame that eventually ignited the logs.

The fire made the inside of the cave glow, giving it a warm and cozy feel.

Liv's body shook for an entirely different reason now.

With just the two of them in the cave, with an intimate fire burning, Liv's imagination went wild.

One glance across the gentle flames into Hawkeye's gaze let her know he might just be thinking along the same lines.

Her heart thundered against her ribs and a fire lit inside her. The night had a whole new set of possibilities.

Chapter Ten

Hawkeye stared across the fire at Olivia, his pulse kicking up several notches.

Her green eyes reflected the flames of the fire burning in the circle. She stood with her hands curled around her elbows. And she was staring at him. Her tongue snaked out to trail across her lower lip.

Holy hell, how was he going to keep his hands off the woman all night long? He'd have to stay awake enough to keep the fire burning, but what he was more concerned about was the desire building like molten lava pressing against the earth's crust. If he didn't find a relief valve soon, that hot lava would erupt and spill all over the interior of the cave and flow right into Olivia.

Somewhere along the way, her long hair had

slipped free of the ponytail. Now it lay in wild disarray around her shoulders and down her back. She looked like a wild, untamed Valkyrie, ready to make her stand.

"I don't suppose you kept a stash of nuts or jerky in that compartment, did you?" Not that he was hungry for food. He'd rather feast on the woman standing before him.

Well, damn. He'd promised himself he wouldn't get involved with a woman again while he was on active duty. One-night stands were okay because he refused to make commitments. Unfortunately, Olivia wasn't the one-night-stand kind of woman.

She deserved better. She needed a man who could work alongside her, help her run the ranch and give her an entire houseful of children.

That man wasn't Hawkeye. With a career in the army, children weren't in the cards for him as long as he was on active duty. War took him away too often, for up to fourteen months at a time. He didn't want any kid of his growing up without a father. And he didn't want the mother of his children to have to raise them alone. Not while running a ranch. That would be impossible. If he were killed in battle, where would that leave his wife? Alone and raising kids without help.

Of course, a man could die from being thrown by a horse, or killed in a car wreck. But he was more likely to be thrown into harm's way in the military. It took a special kind of woman to stand by her man while he was away. And it took a special man to make the sacrifices necessary to do right by his wife and children.

And he was back to the fact that stood out most in his mind—Olivia wasn't a one-night-stand kind of woman.

Which meant he had to keep his hands to himself.

But when she looked at him across the fire, with her soft green eyes so wide and trusting and full of…

Lust?

His pulse hammered in his veins, pushing blood low in his groin.

If he explained it to her, she could make the choice. If she said no, that would be the end of it.

"Olivia," he started, his voice catching. He cleared his throat and rounded the fire pit to stand in front of her. "We should talk."

She nodded. "What do you want to talk about?"

He took her hand in his and stared down at her fingers—so small, yet capable.

The first mistake.

As soon as their skin touched, an electric current zipped through him and couldn't be undone. He lifted her fingers to his lips and pressed a kiss to the backs of her knuckles. "You know I'm here on a temporary basis."

She nodded. "I know."

"I have a career with the army."

Her lips curled slightly upward. "I know that, too."

"Whatever it is we're feeling..."

She stepped closer, bringing their joined hands up, sandwiching them between their bodies. "Go on." Her gaze lifted to his, forcing him to face her, to say what came next.

"I find you very attractive."

She chuckled. "Even when I smell like a horse and my hair is a tangled mess?"

"You've never been more beautiful with the flames emphasizing the fiery red highlights in your hair." He reached up and brushed a strand back from her cheek.

"Are you trying to let me down easy?" she asked, her gaze dropping to his mouth. "Before we've been out on even one date?" She shook her head.

"When this assignment is done, I'll be back with my unit, possibly shipping out to another assignment in the Middle East."

"I know." She leaned up on her toes and brushed his lips with hers. "What's your point?"

"I can't make any commitments." There, he'd said it. He'd more or less told her that anything they might have between them wouldn't last. It was her turn to tell him to take a walk. That she wasn't interested.

"Who said I wanted commitment? I have my own life and my own responsibilities. Besides, we barely know each other."

"I know enough about you to realize you deserve a man who can stick around and help you on your ranch."

She spread her fingers across his chest. "I can hire a ranch hand for that."

"You need a man who will be there for you 24/7."

She tilted her head. "Haven't I told you? I can take care of myself."

He smiled. "Yes, you can. But you deserve someone you can depend on when the going gets tough."

"I have Abe," she countered.

"What I'm saying is— Oh, hell." He sighed and pushed a hand through his hair. "I'm only good for a one-night stand. You deserve better."

"Who said I wanted more?" She traced his jawline with the tip of her finger. "What if I have too much on my plate for anything more?"

Hawkeye groaned. "Do you know how much I want to make love to you?"

She pressed her body to his. "I do now."

He dropped his hands to her hips and pulled her against him, loving the feel of her soft belly against his hardness. "This isn't how I pictured making love to you."

She grinned. "So you've been thinking about it?"

He nodded. "You're an amazing woman. You're strong, independent and sit a horse like you belong there."

She leaned up on her toes and kissed his chin. "I thought you didn't like horses." Then she touched her lips to his in the gentlest of brushes.

"I never said I didn't like horses."

She moved her hips, rubbing against that very sensitive and engorged part of his body.

He drew in a steadying breath. "I'm going to go to hell for this."

She laced her hands at the back of his head. "Then take me with you." Pulling his head down to hers, she kissed him, thrusting her tongue past his teeth to parry with his.

He took her mouth, claiming it as his own, his hands roaming over her shoulders, down her back to the curve of her buttocks. She was strong, passionate and his.

For the moment. And he had no intention of missing out on that moment.

Olivia gave as good as she got, thrusting, twisting and tangling with him. But then, in the middle of the kiss, she stiffened and pulled back. "Please tell me you have protection."

He drew his head back and stared down at her, his brain fogged with lust. "What? Protection?" It took him a full second to realize what she was talking about. Then he remembered he still carried his wallet in his back pocket. He fumbled for it, flipped it open and dug inside until his fingers closed around a foil packet.

He held up the treasure. "We're covered."

"Good, because I can't wait much longer." She unzipped her jacket and let it fall to the floor. Then she flicked the buttons loose on her blouse and pushed it over her shoulders.

While Hawkeye slipped the straps of her bra down Olivia's arms, she shoved his jacket over his shoulders and dropped it to the floor.

Her breasts spilled from the cups of her bra into his hands and he bent to kiss the tips of both, one at a time.

Hawkeye straightened, tugged his T-shirt from the waistband of his jeans and ripped it up over his head. He bent to spread his jacket and T-shirt across the smooth surface of the cave, near the fire. Turning to Olivia, he held out his hand.

She took his and walked to him. "You still have time to back out."

He chuckled. "That's my line."

With a shrug, she reached for the button on his jeans. "Just saying. If you aren't feeling it, don't think you have to go through with this."

"Have you changed your mind?" He caught her hands in his, stilling her fingers from tugging his zipper down.

"No. I'm all in on this adventure."

Hawkeye released her hands.

She slid the zipper down and pushed the jeans over his hips and past his thighs.

His patience stretched too thin, Hawkeye shoved them the rest of the way down, toed off his boots and stepped out of the jeans. The cool night air couldn't begin to chill his desire for the woman standing in front of him.

When she reached for the button on her jeans, he brushed her hands aside and took over. In a slow, steady motion, he lowered the zipper and smoothed her jeans down her gorgeous legs to her ankles. There he helped her out of her boots and jeans, and the cute pink bikini panties that surprised him.

"Pink?"

"I might not be a girlie-girl on the outside, but I like pretty underthings." Olivia cupped his cheeks, leaned up to kiss him and then dragged her lips over his chin and down his neck to his collarbone.

"Sweetheart, you're burning a path right through me." He swept her up into his arms and laid her down on the shirt and jacket, pressing a kiss to the pulse beating wildly at the base of her throat. "Promise me you'll have no regrets."

"The only regret I might have is that you're taking it too slow and easy." She captured his face between her palms. "Foreplay can be entirely overrated. Besides, my body is on fire."

"Are you too close to the flames?"

"You could say that. But the heat has nothing to do with the campfire." She wrapped her leg around the back of his, rubbing her sex against his thigh.

With the fire keeping the chill night air at bay and providing a warm, inviting glow, Hawk-eye knew he wouldn't last long if he took her fast. He wanted her to enjoy their lovemaking as much as he did. For that to happen, he had to take her there, a little at a time.

He dropped down over her, leaning his weight on one arm, his knee nudging her thighs apart.

She spread them wide enough for him to slip between.

He pressed his erection, pulsing and hard, to her entrance and held it there without penetrating. Once again, he claimed her lips, kissing her long and tender, thrusting his tongue between her teeth, mimicking what their bodies would be doing next. "Woman, do you have any idea how much I want you?"

Liv laughed, the sound echoing off the walls of the cave. "Oh, I have a clue." And she was every bit as turned on as he was. If he didn't get moving soon, she would explode into a thousand little pieces.

Olivia gripped his buttocks and pulled him toward her, trying to get him to consummate their lovemaking. She wanted him. Inside her. Now.

He resisted her insistent grasp, refusing to enter. Instead, he slipped lower, sliding his lips down the long column of her throat to the base where the pulse beat so rapidly she was afraid her heart would spontaneously combust.

Moving lower, Hawkeye skimmed over the swell of her breast and stopped at her right nipple, sucking the beaded tip into his mouth. Pulling hard, he tongued, flicked and nibbled it.

Liv arched her back off the floor of the cave, gripped the back of Hawkeye's head and urged him to take more.

He did, taking half of her breast into his mouth. Then he switched to the other and treated it to the same sensuous delights.

A moan escaped her lips. "Oh, please, don't make me wait. I want you inside me."

"When you're ready," he said, his lips trailing a path down her torso to the tuft of hair covering her sex.

"Honey, any more ready and I'll come apart."

He parted her folds and blew a warm stream of air over her heated flesh.

Liv dug her heels into the ground and lifted her hips. She wanted more. Hell, she *needed* more. "Please," she whispered.

Hawkeye bent his head and tongued her there.

A burst of sensations swept over her, the tension inside building, like a bowstring pulled back until it was so taut it might snap. How much more could she take? Liv felt like she teetered on a precipice, her body no longer under her control.

Hawkeye pressed two fingers into her and swirled his tongue over that most sensitive strip of flesh, sending her flying over the edge, jolts of electricity catapulting her into the stratosphere. She dug her fingers into his scalp and lifted her hips, her back straining, her body so tight she couldn't move as wave after wave washed over her.

She rode it all the way to the shore. When she could breathe again, she tugged on Hawkeye's hair, grabbed his shoulder and pulled him up her body. "Now. I need you inside me, now!"

He chuckled, his body sliding against hers,

his hips dropping down between her thighs. "Are you ready?"

"Oh, yes!" She dug her fingernails into his butt cheeks.

"Will you do the honors?" He handed her the foil packet.

She tore it open and rolled it down over him in less time than it took to say *make love to me*.

Then he was pressing into her, his girth stretching her, filling her. He slid deeper, until he could go no farther. For a long, excruciating moment, he paused, letting her channel adjust to his size.

She pushed his hips away.

He let her guide him in the slow, steady strokes.

Liv raised her hips to match his thrusts with ones of her own.

Soon, he took over, bracing his hands on either side of her. He pumped in and out of her, increasing in speed and intensity until he was slamming in and out of her, again and again.

The same sensations rose inside all over again, exploding in a flash of electrical impulses, tingling from her core all the way out to her fingertips and toes.

Hawkeye thrust one last time, burying himself all the way inside her where he remained, his staff throbbing against her channel, his buttocks tight, his face strained.

At last, he collapsed against her and rolled them both to the side, placing her backside to the fire.

Liv lay there for a long time, loving that they were still intimately connected. Being with Hawkcyc gave a whole new meaning to sleeping by the campfire. She could do this again. And again.

With the warmth of the fire behind her and Hawkeye's heat in front, she snuggled close and shut her eyes. "Do you think they will come back and find us tonight?"

"I seriously doubt it. But I'll keep one eye open, just in case."

"Let me know—" she yawned "—if you need another. In the meantime, I'm going to take a little nap. You wore me out."

His chuckle was warm and rich, filling her heart with joy and contentment.

Yeah, she could get used to his laughter and his body cocooning hers. "Thank you."

He laughed again. "You nut. What for?"

"For reminding me why foreplay is so very important."

His still-stiff staff flexed inside her.

Liv draped her leg over his and moved closer. Then she drifted to sleep, not caring that the stone floor of the cave was cold and hard. She was wrapped in the arms of a man who could very easily steal her heart. It was a good thing neither one of them was in the market for commitment. Otherwise, he could also very easily break her heart.

Chapter Eleven

Sunlight filtered in through the cave entrance along with a cool morning breeze. The fire had long since burned out, leaving nothing but fading embers. Gooseflesh made the hairs on Hawkeye's arms stand straight.

He stared down at Olivia, memorizing her straight, perky nose and the swell of her full, sexy lips. Though she wore no makeup, her auburn eyelashes made fiery crescents against her lightly tanned skin as she slept.

He knew that when the time came, he was going to miss this woman who had managed to capture his attention and make a significant chink in the armor he'd erected around his heart.

If only he had more time with her. If only he could take her with him when he left.

But Olivia would hate being an army wife. She'd get tired of following him around the country or world, packing every three or four years, sometimes more often, and moving to places where she wouldn't know anyone.

Finding work was often difficult for wives of service members. Employment opportunities weren't always as available around the posts as they were in less remote locations.

Why was he even contemplating it? He'd only known Olivia for a couple of days.

When you know...you know.

His mother's words echoed in his head. He'd asked her how she'd known his father was the right man for her. She'd smiled and said those words then. She'd loved his father with all of her heart. And she'd loved her children so much, she couldn't live with the knowledge one of them had died. She'd always felt everything more deeply than anyone else.

When you know, you know.

Hawkeye's gaze swept across Olivia's features. She had high cheekbones, smile lines beside her eyes and lips, and a strong chin. And her body...

His own tightened as his gaze traveled over her breasts down to the juncture of her thighs.

Even if he wanted to wake her by making love to her, he didn't have any more protection. He refused to risk the odds. Leaving her pregnant with a ranch to run would be a crappy thing to do. She had enough on her hands to worry about.

Hawkeye slipped from beneath her leg draped over his, stood and dressed in his jeans and boots. His shirt and jacket lay beneath Olivia's beautiful body, and he didn't have the heart to wake her yet.

Instead, he walked to the cave entrance and out into the morning light, careful to look for trouble before revealing himself.

There were no signs of the five gunmen from the evening before. If he and Olivia got going, they could fix that fence and get back in time to have breakfast.

His stomach rumbled loudly as he flexed his arms and back. The hard cave floor had left him stiff and aching.

"Hungry?" a voice called out behind him.

Olivia stood in the opening, her hair rumpled, her jeans and boots pulled on. She worked the buttons on her blouse with her fingers as she blinked in the morning sunlight. "Any sign of them?"

He shook his head. "Not as far as I can tell. We'll have to make our way out of here to see if they're really gone."

"I'm ready when you are." She handed him the T-shirt and jacket he'd worn the day before.

Olivia tucked her shirt into her waistband and finger-combed her hair in an attempt to tame the thick, wavy locks. Finally, she gave up and walked back into the cave.

Hawkeye followed.

She stood next to the four-wheeler. "You can drive. I feel like my arms and legs were pummeled by our ride across the boulders. I'm not sure I can manhandle the handlebars to get us back."

He nodded, certain Olivia could do anything she set her mind to. However, the shadows beneath her eyes told him she hadn't slept any better than he had on the hard ground. He wanted to soothe her aches and make everything all right for her. Hawkeye opened his arms.

For a moment, she hesitated. But then she leaned into him and rested her cheek against his chest. "I hate that I don't feel safe anymore."

"Stay with me. I'll do my best to protect you."

She shook her head. "I can't get used to having you around. When you leave, I'm on my own again. I might as well get used to it now."

"By then, we will have figured out the problems here. I'm not going anywhere until everything is settled."

She glanced up at him. "What if it takes a long time?"

He brushed his lips across her nose. "Then we will have more time together." His brows furrowed. "Seriously. I'm not leaving until I know you're safe."

She wrapped her arms around his waist. "I'm glad. I'm sure I can take care of myself, but you were right. I like having someone watching my back."

He rested his cheek against her riotous hair. "You've got me, babe." Until he left. The more he thought about that day, the less he liked it. Even if they settled the troubles and figured out who was responsible for the guns and the killings, there could always be another bad guy to take the place of the ones they cleaned up. Olivia would be on her own with only Abe as her backup. And Abe wasn't getting any younger.

For the first time since he'd enlisted in the

army, Hawkeye thought about what he'd do if he wasn't a soldier anymore.

He could go back to ranching. It was in his blood. Maybe he could hire on as a ranch hand on the Stone Oak Ranch. Then he could be close enough to Olivia to help her out when she got into a pinch. Or he could hire on with the sheriff's department. He had the skills. He'd only need to go through the training to learn all of the nuances of local laws. Or he could ask Kevin Garner for a job as a permanent member of his Homeland Security team.

Ah, who was he kidding? It was hard enough adjusting to the civilian world on a temporary assignment. He'd been in the military for so long, he wasn't sure he could transition out of it permanently. He inhaled the scent of Olivia. Although the civilian world had its perks.

Hawkeye's arms tightened around her. "Ready to go?"

"No." She hugged him harder and then sighed, her arms loosening. "If we must. The fence still needs mending and the animals will need to be fed and watered."

"I'd bet my socks CJ has the barn animals under control."

Olivia smiled. "He's a good kid. I just hate that his stepfather is a jerk."

"You and me both." Hawkeye climbed aboard the four-wheeler and waited for Olivia to mount behind him. Then he eased out of the cave entrance and half drove, half slid down the hill to the rocky bottom.

They wove through the big boulders until they reached the trail headed back to the ranch.

Hawkeye paused for a moment and looked back at the many caves lining the bluffs. "I'll have Garner send some of the other team members back this way to check out the other caves. The weapons cache has to be around here somewhere."

The ride back to the mangled fence passed uneventfully.

As soon as they crossed back onto Stone Oak Ranch land, Olivia hopped off the four-wheeler and whistled loudly for her horse. An answering whinny made her smile. She ran toward a stand of bushes where she found Stormy's reins tangled in a thorny briar vine. Stormy stamped his hooves impatiently while Olivia and Hawkeye pulled the leather free of the prickly plant.

Once free, the gelding tossed his head and nuzzled Olivia, searching for a treat.

"Sorry, old boy. We have to fix this fence before we go back to the barn." She tied him to a low-hanging tree branch and joined Hawkeye.

He loved watching her work with animals. She had patience and a true affinity for them. Olivia showed she cared by the way she treated them and the way they responded to her.

Hawkeye tacked the end of the barbed wire to a fence post and unwound a strand long enough to fill the gap where the fence had been cut. Using the come-along, he and Olivia quickly strung fresh barbed wire in four rows and tacked the wire to the fence posts with the staples. The job only took an hour and then they were loaded up and heading back to the ranch house before the sun had fully risen in the sky.

Again, Hawkeye trailed Olivia and her horse, giving the gelding enough room that he wasn't spooked by the noise from the engine.

Next time, Hawkeye vowed to take a horse if Olivia insisted on riding one. At least then he'd be able to hear the sound of engines before the gang riding the ATVs caught them in their sights. Following behind Olivia wasn't all bad. The woman sat her horse beautifully, swaying with every step, as much a part of the animal as the animal itself.

She hadn't mentioned their lovemaking, which made him wonder if she was now regretting it. If that were the case, he'd be disappointed. He'd already envisioned a night with Olivia in a real bed, not on the hard surface of the cave floor. Call him selfish and lacking focus, but Hawkeye couldn't help it. The woman had his libido tied in knots.

LIV'S TENDER PARTS were sore that morning as she eased into the saddle. Having Hawkeye follow her back to the ranch made her hyperaware of his gaze on her backside.

She'd wanted to wake in his arms, but he'd been up and outside before she woke from an uneasy sleep. Liv had hoped they'd pick up where they'd left off the night before. But then she remembered he'd only brought protection for one round.

A trip to town would remedy that shortfall for future encounters with the gorgeous army ranger.

Crap! What if they didn't carry such protection in the grocery store? Would they have them in the feed store? If she had to, she'd drive all the way to Bozeman, Montana, for them.

As long as Hawkeye was in town, she hoped

to continue relations with the man. When it came time for him to leave, she'd just have to remind herself she'd agreed to the no-commitment clause.

Her chest tightened at the thought of Hawkeye leaving. Hopefully, his little team would be around for a lot longer. Although she'd like to solve the mystery of who was doing all the killing as soon as possible—before someone else turned up dead.

Liv swung out of the saddle at the gate to the barnyard and unlatched the lock.

"CJ?" she called out as she led Stormy through and waited for Hawkeye to drive the ATV in behind her.

The barn door swung open and CJ emerged carrying the rifle from the tack room. "Oh, thank goodness, it's you two." He lowered the weapon and sighed. "If you hadn't turned up by nine o'clock, I was going to call the sheriff."

"We're all right, but thanks for worrying about us." Liv led Stormy into the barn.

Hawkeye killed the engine on the four-wheeler and pushed it into the barn behind her.

"How long have you been here?" Liv called out over her shoulder.

CJ had ducked into the tack room to hang the

rifle on the wall. He rejoined them, stretched and yawned before answering, "All night."

Liv spun. "All night?"

"I left long enough to do my chores at home. As soon as I could, I snuck out and came back to make sure someone watched over the house and barn in case you didn't make it back before dark. I was worried about you."

Liv hugged the teen. "Oh, CJ. I'm sorry. I hope you didn't stay awake all night."

He shrugged. "I can catch up on my sleep later."

"Why were you up all night?" Hawkeye asked.

The boy's brows furrowed. "I was sleeping in the barn, but something woke me in the middle of the night. Sadly, a little late for me to do much about it, but, heck, you'll have to see this for yourself."

Liv tied Stormy to a metal ring on the wall and followed CJ outside and up the hill to the house.

"The horses and cattle out in the pasture were making a lot of noise. I thought maybe a wolf or a bear had found its way into the pens. I grabbed the gun from the tack room thinking I could fire into the air and scare it off. But when I came out of the barn, I saw someone moving around the house."

They'd arrived at the house and swung around to the front.

A chill slithered down the back of Liv's neck. She and Hawkeye had been gone all night. "You didn't try to confront him, did you?" CJ could have been attacked and injured or killed. She glanced over the boy's head to Hawkeye.

The ranger's brows had dropped into a deep frown as he stared toward the house.

Her stomach churning, Olivia's gaze followed Hawkeye's.

There on the front of the house in huge bloodred scrawl across the white paint and the glass of the windows were the words "LEAVE OUR SACRED LANDS."

"I'm sorry I couldn't stop him sooner," CJ said. "I fired off a round. It must have scared whoever it was, because he disappeared down the driveway. I heard the sound of a vehicle engine, but by the time I chased after him, he was gone."

Liv wrapped her arm around the teen. "Oh, CJ, no. You shouldn't have chased him at all. Dear Lord, I would never forgive myself if something bad happened to you."

He stood taller, his shoulders thrown back. "I had the rifle. The shot I fired into the air scared him away."

Hugging the boy again, Olivia felt her stomach knot. What if the man who'd spray painted her house had come after CJ?

"Why would they paint this message?" Hawkeye asked. He turned to Olivia. "Have you had troubles with the local Native American tribes in the past?"

Liv shook her head. "Never. As far back as I can remember, we haven't encountered any disputes over the property. We border the national forest, not a reservation."

Hawkeye crossed his arms over his chest, still studying the scrawled words on the wall as if they might shed more light. "Are there any ancient burial grounds on Stone Oak Ranch?"

"Not that I'm aware of." The warning made no sense. "My father has always had a good relationship with just about everyone in the county and on the nearby reservation. He donated whole steers to them to help feed people during some of the more trying times."

Hawkeye turned away from the house and stared at the yard surrounding it. "Look around.

See if you can find the spray can. Maybe we can lift prints from it."

The three of them split up, combing over the lawn, the shrubs and the tree line several yards away.

"I found it!" CJ called out.

"Don't touch it," Hawkeye said.

The two adults converged on CJ and stared down at the empty can of red spray paint.

"I'll get a paper bag from the kitchen." Liv ran around the back of the house and entered through the kitchen door. She dug through the pantry until she found an old paper grocery bag. After grabbing it, she ran back out into the yard.

Hawkeye nudged the can with his foot, pushing it into the paper bag without touching it with his own hands. Once the can was safely inside the bag, he lifted it, folded the top and carried it back to the house.

"I'll call the sheriff." Liv went to the phone and dialed the sheriff's office, reporting the vandalism.

By the time she got off the phone, she could smell bacon cooking in the kitchen. Her stomach rumbled, reminding her she hadn't had anything to eat since breakfast the previous morning.

But more than food, she wanted a shower to wash the scent of the campfire out of her hair and off her skin.

Leaving the men to the kitchen, she sneaked away to her room for fresh clothing and ducked into the bathroom for a shower. A few minutes later she was clean, combed and dressed in freshly laundered jeans and a T-shirt.

When she stepped out of the bathroom, she heard voices coming from the hallway.

Sheriff Scott stood with Hawkeye and CJ. All three turned when she joined them.

"Miss Dawson." Sheriff Scott enveloped her in a bear hug. "I'm sorry about the vandalism to your house. We'll do our best to find out who did this and make him clean it up and hopefully keep him from doing it again." He shook his head. "And about the gang who chased you in the hills... I'll have my deputies do some asking around. Attempted murder is serious business. If you could swing by the office and give me your statement later today, I'd appreciate it."

"You bet, Sheriff." Liv hugged the older man again. "Thank you for all of your help."

"Glad you're back," the sheriff said. "Your

dad missed you something fierce." He shook his head. "I was really sorry about his passing. He was a good man."

She drew in a deep breath and lifted her chin a little. "Did anyone suspect his death might not have been an accident?"

The sheriff tilted his head to the side and considered her question. "With so many strange things going on, we haven't ruled it out. But we didn't have any witnesses and the only person we knew to question was Abe, who wasn't anywhere near your father at the time. Don't worry, though. We haven't given up."

Liv nodded. "Thanks, Sheriff. I don't suppose you'd like to join us for breakfast?"

He shook his head. "No, thanks." He patted his belly. "The wife keeps me fat and happy."

After the sheriff left, Liv joined Hawkeye and CJ in the kitchen. She ate the eggs, bacon and toast Hawkeye had whipped up, enjoying every bite. After she'd cleaned her plate, she sat back. "I need to remember to hire someone who can cook as well as you do when I'm looking for a ranch hand."

Hawkeye's jaw tightened, but he didn't respond to her statement. "I'd like to make a trip into town after we finish the chores around here."

"Okay. Are we going to see your boss?"

He nodded. "I'll give him a call with a heads-up on what's been going on. He'll need to know what happened yesterday. It might be connected with your father in some way."

CJ cleared the table of the plates and returned for the glasses. "You know, there's a gang at the res that likes to ride dirt bikes and ATVs all over the place. Sometimes they get into trouble."

Liv pushed her chair away from the table and stood. "Why didn't you tell the sheriff?"

"I wasn't sure it was the gang and I'd hate to get them into trouble if it wasn't." He took the glasses to the sink and rinsed them before loading them into the dishwasher. "I wouldn't want them to know I was the person who ratted them out."

Chapter Twelve

Hawkeye understood CJ's wanting to stay quiet.

Olivia looked at him over the boy's head.

Hawkeye's lips pressed together and he gave her a slight nod. "I'll have Garner ask around. He might have more luck getting information than an officer of the local law enforcement."

CJ faced them. "You won't tell them you got that lead from me?"

Hawkeye smiled. "No. Your secret is safe with us."

"Thanks." He wiped the counter and headed for the door. "I'll work on removing the red paint today, after I finish my chores in the barn."

"Don't worry about it, CJ," Olivia said. "I think I can get it off. If not, my father stored touch-up paint in the basement. And thanks, CJ. I don't know what I'd do without you around."

The teen's cheeks reddened and he ducked out the door.

"If you don't mind, I'll use the phone in the hallway," Hawkeye said.

"Please. Make yourself at home." She snorted softly. "Funny, but this house hasn't felt much like home since I returned."

"Your family isn't here," Hawkeye said. "Family is what makes a house a home."

She nodded. "Though I resisted at first, I'm glad you stuck around."

"Why's that?"

Olivia shrugged. "As much as I hate to admit it, you make me feel safer."

"Glad I could help." He would have said more, but he still wasn't sure what good he would be to her once he was gone. Hawkeye left the kitchen, headed for the hall, anxious to report in to Garner.

His temporary boss answered on the first ring. "Garner."

"Hawkeye here. We had a little incident last night."

"Shoot."

After describing the encounter in the valley

and their subsequent campout in a cave, minus a few more personal details, Hawkeye paused. "And that's not all. We got back to the Dawson house to some threatening graffiti sprayed on the front of the ranch house. Olivia's ranch hand nearly caught the man in the act, but he got away."

"I thought her ranch hand was in the hospital?"

Hawkeye grinned. "She hired CJ Running Bear to help out while her foreman is laid up."

"Glad she found some help. Wait. Isn't CJ Ernie Martin's stepson? The teen working in the kitchen at the tavern?"

"Not anymore. His stepfather made him quit."

Garner muttered a curse. "Poor kid. I feel for him. Martin has a nasty temper."

"Yeah. We were there when he threw the kid out of the tavern."

"So that's what all of that was about? I heard the scuffle, but it was over by the time I came outside. I'm glad Miss Dawson could use CJ. Ernie Martin is in serious trouble financially. He hawked his house to purchase Angora goats right before the government ceased the subsidies on them. He has no way to pay back the loans and he's not making enough money on his ranch to feed his family."

"All reasons to be angry enough to join a survivalist organization. Is it enough to make him a killer?" Hawkeye couldn't be sure. Though, as mean as Ernie had been to CJ, Hawkeye wouldn't put it past him to take it one step further.

"Hard to say," Garner said. "We'll check into his alibi for the afternoon Dawson died."

"Might be worth looking into," Hawkeye said. "Anything from Hack?"

"As a matter of fact, I was about to call you." Garner spoke as if talking to someone else in the room. "Could you bring me that printout we were discussing?"

Hawkeye waited.

"Hack checked into the names you gave us. Leo Fratiani checks out as a land agent for one of the big oil companies. Hack is still digging, trying to see if he's connected to anything that raises any red flags besides the oil industry, as if that isn't enough. Morris's record is a bit too clean. Hack will be digging much deeper."

"He has to have a fairly clean record to run for Congress." Hawkeye's eyes narrowed. "Is there a way to cleanse your background?"

"If there is," Garner said, "he's found it. I'm talking squeaky clean."

"What about Bryson Rausch? Any skeletons in his closet?" Hawkeye asked.

"Nothing more than the fact he owns about half of the buildings in Grizzly Pass and is always looking for more real estate to gobble up."

Which matched up with Olivia's description of the man.

Garner continued. "Sweeney has us concerned."

The tone of Garner's voice had Hawkeye's attention. "Why?"

"That man's bad news. He was kicked out of the Marine Corps with a dishonorable discharge. Spent some time at Leavenworth before he was discharged for raping an Afghan woman."

A knot of tension settled low in Hawkeye's gut. "Bastard. Does he have to register as a sex offender?"

"You bet he does," Garner said. "That's how Hack found out Sweeney had been kicked out of the Corps. His first hit on the guy was that he'd been marked as a sex offender and has to register in whatever county he lives. Then Hack found his way into the man's military records and discovered his court-martial for the rape of the Afghan woman."

"That's not what I wanted to hear, but it's better to know than not."

"Right," Garner agreed.

"We sent the spray can used to vandalize the Dawson house with the sheriff," Hawkeye said. "He's going to see if he can lift prints. Let us know if you hear anything before we do."

"I'll touch base with the sheriff right now. You two need to grow eyes in the backs of your heads and stay safe."

"Will do." As Hawkeye hung up, Olivia walked into the hallway.

"Has he heard anything about the people you asked him to check up on?" Liv asked.

Hawkeye held out his hand.

Liv placed hers in his and he pulled her up against his body. She fit him perfectly. Leaving her and Grizzly Pass would be really hard when the time came.

"Yeah, he did have some news. Not much on Morris, Rausch or Fratiani."

"What about Don Sweeney?" Liv raised her face to his.

Hawkeye brushed a strand of her hair back behind her ear. "He did say Sweeney had a record."

"Oh?"

He told her what Garner had said about the rape charge and his dishonorable discharge.

Liv's face hardened and her lips thinned into a straight line. "It's men like him we don't want coming back home to live in Grizzly Pass."

"And, yes, he has to register as a sex offender."

"A real piece of work." Liv's gut tightened. "I'll be sure to steer clear of him and let the other women in the county know to stay away."

"One other thing that has come up before in our investigation of what's been going on around the area." Hawkeye paused. "Sweeney along with Ernie Martin and a couple other locals are suspected members of the Free America organization."

"You'd think, with his record, Sweeney wouldn't be allowed to join such an organization." Liv laid her cheek against Hawkeye's chest.

He stroked her hair and down her back, his groin tightening the longer she pressed against him. He was so caught up in what her nearness was doing to his body, Hawkeye almost forgot what Olivia had said.

He pulled his focus back to the issue. "The Free America group is secret. We still don't know who is leading it or is funding its arsenal." He leaned her back far enough to press a gentle kiss to her healing forehead. "I'm worried about you."

She stared up into his eyes. "I'm worried about all of the good people of Grizzly Pass. I always thought this was a good place to live and raise a family. And it used to be just that." Liv shook her head. "And it was that for a very long time."

"It's a shame that a few people can bring chaos to an entire community." He bent to touch his lips to hers. "Part of me is glad it happened."

Liv opened her eyes wider, her lips full and inviting him to kiss them. "What did you say? You're glad?"

"If this part of the country wasn't in trouble, Garner wouldn't have asked for help from the military. I would never have been assigned to assist the Department of Homeland Security."

"And we would never have met," Liv whispered.

"Exactly." This time Hawkeye took her mouth, her tongue and crushed her to him.

Liv wrapped her arms around his neck

and returned the gesture, coiling her tongue around his.

Hawkeye lost himself in the kiss, becoming a part of her in the process. When he finally brought his head up, he stared down into her eyes. His heart pounded in his chest, and his desire welled up inside so hot and fast he felt like Old Faithful seconds before it blew. Hawkeye held himself rigid, afraid to move. Afraid he'd take her there in the hallway. "I didn't think it could get any better than making love to you in a cave. But I could be wrong."

"We could test the theory. Now." Olivia tilted her head toward her bedroom. "In a real bed."

"You don't know how much I want that." Hawkeye drew in a deep breath and let it out slowly, shaking his head. "But not without protection."

Olivia sighed. "I hate it when you're right."

So did he. With everything else going on, Olivia couldn't afford to get pregnant. Who would take care of the ranch if she was knocked up?

Telling himself he could wait didn't make him any less anxious to strip her and make love to her. But he had to remain in control. Especially when Olivia was in danger.

She rested her forehead against his chest for a moment, seeming to get a grip on her rising passion. Then she pushed away from him. "So where do we go from here?"

He squared his shoulders and nodded toward the front of the house. "To work."

For the next couple of hours, Olivia scraped graffiti off the windows and applied several coats of paint to cover the dark red lettering on the siding.

Hawkeye banished himself to the barn to help CJ organize the hay in the loft. He came out periodically to check on Olivia's progress, offering to take over and finish the restoration.

Olivia refused, stating this was something she wanted to do herself. "The house, the ranch and everything on it was a source of pride to my father. The least I can do is restore the house to honor him."

A little after noon, Olivia had disappeared inside the house.

Hawkeye laid the last bale of hay in the neat stack they'd made in the corner of the loft and straightened his aching body. The pain in his lower back reminded him how hard work on the ranch could be. But it was also rewarding to see the results of his and CJ's efforts. He clapped a hand to the teen's back. "Good job."

The boy's belly grumbled and he pressed his palm to his midsection.

Hawkeye laughed. "Let's see if Miss Dawson has something in mind for lunch."

CJ shot a narrow-eyed glance at Hawkeye. "I didn't think she could cook. You're always the one making breakfast."

"True. But maybe we underestimate her." He led the way down the steps to the ground floor of the barn and out to the water hose in the barnyard. He turned on the water and ducked his head beneath the stream, washing out the sweat and hay dust.

When he was done, he held out the hose to CJ. "Your turn."

When they were sufficiently washed up, they headed to the back door and knocked.

"Lunch is ready," Olivia called out.

Hawkeye held the door for CJ and he entered.

Olivia had laid sandwiches on the table along with chips and a pitcher of lemonade.

"I told you she could cook." Hawkeye winked at CJ.

"Making a sandwich is not the same as cooking," CJ said, beneath his breath.

Olivia planted her fists on her hips. "I can cook. Just not with a stove." She laughed. "Stoves and I have a love/hate relationship."

"How's that?" Hawkeye asked, holding a chair out for Olivia and then sitting beside her.

CJ took the seat on the opposite side of the table.

Olivia smiled. "I hate using them, but love what others are able to accomplish with them." She waved her hand at the table. "Eat up, unless you want to cook something else. In which case, I'd like to add my order to your efforts."

"Peanut butter and jelly sounds great." CJ lifted his sandwich and took a big bite.

Hawkeye followed suit.

When they'd finished off their lunch, Hawkeye patted his belly and grinned. "Reminds me of summers at home."

CJ licked the jelly off his fingers and glanced up. "Speaking of home, I need to check in. My mother will be worried that I wasn't there this morning."

"You're welcome to use the telephone and call her."

"Can't." The boy's face was grim. "They cut off our telephone service."

"Cut off?" Olivia frowned.

CJ blushed and looked away. "Ernie didn't pay the bill."

Olivia stood. "If you need an advance on your wages, I can do that."

The teen's cheeks grew even redder. "No. You've done enough just giving me this job." He hopped up from the table and cleared their dishes. Once he had the kitchen clean, he was out the door.

Hawkeye followed Olivia out onto the porch.

She leaned against the rail and waved at CJ driving off on the scooter. "I think I embarrassed him."

"I'd like to help him more."

"Me, too." She sighed and then straightened. "I need a few groceries from town. You don't have to come if you don't want to." For some strange reason, her cheeks turned a rosy pink.

"I'll drive."

"I don't want to put the miles on your truck." She entered the house and grabbed her purse from the counter. "Really, I can do this on my own."

"I don't mind," he insisted, though he could

swear she was trying to get rid of him. The way things had been going, he didn't want to let her out of his sight for long. "Give me a minute to shower and I'll be ready."

"Sure. I guess that will be okay. I'll just lock up." With the color high in her cheeks, she sailed past him.

He hurried out to his truck, grabbed his duffel bag and returned. Five minutes in the shower, then dressing in a fresh pair of jeans and a T-shirt, and he was ready.

He found Olivia on the porch, where she stared out at the horses in the pasture.

"Ready?" he said.

She nodded, the color in her cheeks back to normal.

They spent the drive into town in silence.

"I'll get the groceries," Olivia said as Hawkeye pulled into the parking lot of the only grocery store in town. "Why don't you check in with your boss? I'll be at least fifteen minutes."

He glanced at the store and then across the street to the tavern. "Are you sure you'll be all right?"

She laughed. "I'll be fine. Nothing's going to happen in broad daylight."

He frowned. "That's what we thought when the kids were hijacked on the bus."

"I'm not a busload of children, and I'll be within shouting distance." Olivia shook her head. "Really, I'll be all right. I want to talk with the store owner in private. She tends to be a wealth of information. If there's gossip, she'll be the first to spread it."

"I've heard that before. Would that be Mrs. Penders?"

Olivia grinned. "The one and only."

He thought about it. What could it hurt? He would be across the street, watching the store from the upstairs apartment window. "Okay. But fifteen minutes and then I'm coming to find you."

She stuck out her hand. "Deal."

He took it and jerked her into his arms. "Seal it with a kiss?"

"I like the way you think." Olivia kissed him hard and long, her tongue dueling with his. She wrapped her hands around the back of his neck and pulled him closer, until the truck console dug into his side.

When she finally let go, he took a ragged breath. "How about we head back to the ranch and finish that kiss?"

She touched his cheek and winked. "After I get the groceries." Then she jumped out of the truck and hustled toward the store entrance.

Hawkeye took a little longer getting out of the vehicle. He had to adjust his jeans to relieve the pressure inside. The woman was making more of an impression on him by the minute. He doubted he would escape Grizzly Pass without feeling like he'd left something important behind.

His thoughts swirling around Olivia and that kiss, Hawkeye crossed the street and climbed the stairs to the loft apartment and knocked once before entering.

Kevin met him at the door and shot a glance over his shoulder. "Where's Miss Dawson?"

"At the grocery store." Where he wanted to be at that moment, pinning her to the door of a giant refrigerator to finish that kiss.

"I just got off the phone with the sheriff. They got a match on those prints."

"Already?"

"They didn't have to go far. The prints belong to Ernie Martin."

A lead weight settled in Hawkeye's gut. As if CJ didn't have enough going wrong with his family. His stepfather would likely get jail time or a heavy fine he couldn't pay, and the man would blame it all on CJ. Hawkeye pushed his hand through his hair and walked to the window to stare down at the store on the other side of the street. "Why do you suppose he painted 'leave our sacred lands'?"

"My bet is he was trying to scare Miss Dawson off the ranch and wants to lay the blame on people from the reservation."

"Why?"

"I don't know." Garner stood beside Hawkeye.

"I also had Ghost check out the gang at the reservation. They had an alibi for yesterday afternoon. They were playing basketball at the recreation center on the res at the time you two were being chased. There were plenty of witnesses."

"If not the reservation gang, who could it have been?"

"My bet is some of the Free America recruits." Garner tapped his fingers on the table. "There's something else you need to know."

Hawkeye turned toward Garner.

"Before he'd gotten the word on the latent prints, the sheriff had one of his deputies go back out to where he suspected the getaway vehicle might have been parked in case the perpetrator dropped any other evidence or left any tire tracks. He found a five-gallon jug of gasoline, lying in the ditch along the highway near the Stone Oak Ranch gate. It was as if it might have been thrown there. It was still full of gasoline. We got the fingerprints off it, as well."

The heaviness in Hawkeye's gut turned over and twisted his nerves in a knot. Had he intended to burn the house down? No one but the five guys on the four-wheelers would have known Olivia wouldn't be in her house that night. Hawkeye shifted his attention back to the store, feeling more and more like he needed to cross the street early and make sure Olivia was okay. "Ernie again?"

"No."

Hawkeye's gaze shot to Garner. "No?"

"They got a match on Don Sweeney."

"Damn." Hawkeye clenched his fists. "Tell me the sheriff took him into custody."

The Homeland Security agent shook his head. "He disappeared. Same with Ernie Martin."

Hawkeye spun on his heel and sprinted for the door.

"Where are you going?" Garner asked.

"To the store, to check on Olivia."

Chapter Thirteen

Once Olivia entered the store, she couldn't escape the chatty Mrs. Penders.

The gray-haired woman, wearing an apron with the store name embroidered across the left breast, came out from behind the counter and hugged her. "Olivia, darling. I'm so sorry about your father. He was always such a gentleman and did so much for everyone around here."

"Thank you, Mrs. Penders. I appreciate your kind words." Olivia hugged the store owner, her eyes stinging all over again. She'd never get used to the fact her father wouldn't be home when she returned. Most everyone in Grizzly Pass had been so nice to her, but it didn't help ease the pain. She'd rather have her father back than all of the condolences in the state of Wyoming.

Mrs. Penders leaned back and stared into Liv's face. "I still can't believe they called it an accident."

Liv nodded. "My father was one of the best horsemen in the county. He rode broncos in the rodeo before he met my mother."

Mrs. Penders smiled. "He was always such a handsome man." Then she shook her head and her lips thinned. "No. I don't think he fell off his horse. Someone had to have hit him. I just won't accept that a man who could win so much on the rodeo circuit would fall off a horse to his death."

"If everyone loved my father so much, why would someone want to kill him?" Liv asked the woman who heard every rumor in the little community.

Mrs. Penders leaned closer. "I think it has to do with that darned oil pipeline."

"The pipeline has been there for years. Why would it be a problem now?"

"*Because* it's been there for years. It's getting old. They'll want to replace it soon." Mrs. Penders rounded the counter and leaned on the surface. "It's big business. It could mean a lot of money to the company that lands the contract and a lot of jobs to the locals if they start over."

"Why don't they just repair the old pipeline? It would be a lot less expensive."

"Some argue that the old pipeline runs through some of the most unstable land in North America." Mrs. Penders paused for Liv to make the connection.

"Yellowstone?"

The older woman smiled and nodded. "Some people think an explosion on the pipeline would cause the supervolcano beneath Yellowstone National Park to wake up. They think it would be the end of the world, or at least this part of the world, if that should happen."

Liv shook her head. "That's ridiculous. The chances of that happening in our lifetime are really slim."

"There are people who think otherwise."

"So what does all of this have to do with Stone Oak Ranch?" Liv asked.

"It's rumored the new pipeline will be located farther south to avoid much of the Yellowstone Caldera. And if that's the case, it might be headed through Stone Oak Ranch." She leaned even closer. "You could be sitting on a gold mine. You could sell the ranch for ten times more than it's worth if the pipeline goes through."

"I don't want to sell my ranch," Liv said.

"Well, you could sell the part they want and have enough money to retire on."

"You think someone killed my father for the land the oil company *might* build a pipeline on?" Her stomach roiled at the thought. Her father was dead because of someone's greed. All because he stood in the way of a pipeline deal? "None of this makes sense. And what has the Native Americans upset?"

"If they take the pipeline farther south, it will cut across the corner of the reservation. They're afraid a break in the pipeline could contaminate their water supply."

"The old pipeline could do that, too. Those rivers and streams flow across the reservation."

"They want to shut down the pipeline altogether."

Liv's chest tightened. Hawkeye had caught someone trying to set off a stick of dynamite at a point along the pipeline. It could have been someone from the reservation trying to prove a point, or someone wanting the pipeline work to start up again, thus giving locals the jobs they so desperately needed.

Liv's gut clenched and churned. "What a mess."

Mrs. Penders reached for Liv's hand and gave

it a squeeze. "Oh, honey. It seems like it's nothing but gloom and doom. But I'm sure it will all work out."

"I'm glad we have optimists like you, Mrs. Penders." Liv smiled and glanced around. "I guess I better get my groceries and let you get back to work."

"Let me know if I can help you with anything."

"Thank you." Liv couldn't imagine Mrs. Penders being any more helpful than she'd already been.

Could Kevin Garner know all about this? As the resident agent for the Department of Homeland Security, he should have his pulse on all of the factions stirring up trouble in the area. Pipeline corporations, activists protesting them, Native Americans in the line of fire and a survivalist organization tired of big government calling the shots. What more could go wrong?

Liv didn't want to tempt fate by asking the question aloud. Instead, she hurried to the pharmaceutical aisle where she found a small selection of what she'd originally come to the store to find. She studied the offerings closely, trying to determine what would be the best brand and the most comfortable for both her and Hawkeye. All the while she felt guilty for thinking about her own pleasure when her home was in the middle of a potential firestorm of warring factions.

"If it helps, I run out of this brand before any of the others."

Olivia jumped back, dropping the box in her hand.

Mrs. Penders stood behind her, pointing at the box Olivia hadn't selected. "But I believe one brand is just as effective as the others."

Heat flooded Olivia's cheeks. "Oh, thank you, Mrs. Penders. I was looking for a f-friend."

Mrs. Penders gave her a knowing smile. "Right." The bell over the front door of the store rang, indicating another customer had arrived. "Let me know if you need help with anything else." The older woman hurried back to the register at the front of the store, leaving Liv to suffer her mortification in private.

After grabbing the box she'd dropped on the floor, she replaced it on the shelf and reached for the one Mrs. Penders had pointed out. Liv laid it in the plastic basket she carried and hurried to the back of the store where the refrigerators held the milk, eggs and orange juice. At the rate the three of them were going through the breakfast food, they'd be out of supplies in the next day or two.

Liv heard a loud sound as if a shelf of canned goods had been knocked over, the cans clattering across the floor.

"Mrs. Penders?" Liv stood on her toes, trying to see over the aisles of cereal boxes and laundry detergent.

"Mrs. Penders took a short break," a voice said beside her.

Don Sweeney stepped out of an aisle and blocked her path.

Liv's pulse leaped. She faced the man in front of her, while searching for an escape route in her peripheral vision. "I'll just check and make sure." She tried to step around the scary ex-marine with the unshaven face and tattoos inked across his forearms, but he moved to the side, blocking her path again.

Though she was quaking on the inside, she lifted her chin and gave the man her toughest stare. "Is there something you want, Mr. Sweeney?"

He nodded. "You to come with me. No fuss, no screaming, just come quietly."

The slither of apprehension turned into full-fledged fear. But she couldn't let it get the better of her and she couldn't let it show. A man like Sweeney would feed on her weakness. "Sorry. I have no desire to go anywhere with you." She tried again to step around him.

When he moved in front of her, she darted to the opposite side and dived past him.

For a moment, she thought she'd made it when his hand shot out and snagged her arm, gripping it so tightly it would definitely leave a bruise.

A bruise was the least of Liv's worries. If this man was a known rapist, he could do a lot more than bruise her. At twice her weight and size, he could toss her around like a rag doll and she'd be unable to stop him.

She had to use her brain and think her way out of this situation. And quickly. Mrs. Penders could be lying in a pool of her own blood. The older woman needed help.

"Let go of me," Liv said, her tone stronger and more confident than she felt. "Or I'll scream."

"No, you won't." He clamped his hand on her arm so hard, the pain nearly brought her to her knees. "Not if you want the boy to live."

She stopped resisting immediately. "What boy?"

"Your new hired hand. The Indian brat."

"CJ?" Anger boiled to the surface. "What have you done to CJ?"

"Nothing yet, but I'll kill him if you don't come with me now, quietly."

"How do I know you have him?" She glared at the man. "You could be lying."

"I caught him on the road, riding that stupid scooter you gave him." He sneered at Liv. "Then again, I'd be doing his mama a favor by taking one more kid off her hands. She'd have one less brat to feed."

Liv flew at the man with her free hand and slapped his face so hard it left a big red handprint on his cheek. "You leave that boy alone. He's done nothing to hurt you."

"He nearly shot me. That's enough reason to kill the little bastard."

"You were the one who vandalized my house!" She spit in his face. "That was my father's house."

"Yeah, and if you hadn't come home, I wouldn't need to burn it to the ground with you inside." He yanked her toward him and crushed her to his chest. "But this way, I might have a little fun first."

With her arms pinned to her sides in his iron grasp, she couldn't move to twist her way out.

She kicked his shins, but it didn't seem to faze him in the least.

Sweeney strode through the back storeroom to the loading dock at the rear where a black pickup was parked.

Liv fought and kicked, knowing if she didn't break free, she wouldn't live to make love one more time with Hawkeye. She wouldn't be there to take care of the ranch that had always been her home. She wouldn't marry and have children to leave that ranch to as their heritage.

When Sweeney set her on her feet beside the truck, Liv pretended to faint, letting her body go completely limp.

Braced to fight with her, Sweeney wasn't prepared for her to slip to the ground.

He lost his grip on her and let her fall all the way to the pavement.

Once she cleared his hands, she dived beneath the truck and would have made it if he hadn't grabbed her ankle and pulled her out with one hard jerk. The ex-marine clutched a handful of her hair and dragged her to her feet.

Liv twisted and swung her arms, her fist catching Sweeney in the face.

He grunted, shoved her against the side of the truck and punched her in the jaw.

The force of the blow snapped her head back and it hit the truck. Stars swam before her eyes and pain shot through her jaw all the way back to the base of her skull. Gray fog closed in from all sides. She fought it, willing herself to stay upright, but she couldn't avoid the abyss sucking her into its void.

HAWKEYE REACHED THE door of the grocery store at a full sprint. When he hit the swinging door he expected it to open. It didn't and he slammed his forehead into the glass. He staggered backward and shook his head.

"What the heck?"

The next time he tried the door, he pushed the opposite side. Neither of the double swinging glass doors opened. He pressed his face to the window and looked inside, his blood going cold in his veins.

A shelf of cans lay spilled on the floor and a woman's leg lay sprawled across the tiles, sticking out from behind the cash-register stand.

Fear ripped through Hawkeye. The absolute certainty that something horrible had happened to Olivia filled him with dread. He turned his body and hit the door with his shoulder. Again he bounced back. The locks keeping the doors in place held true.

"What's wrong?" Garner joined him on the sidewalk.

"The door's locked and someone is lying on the floor inside. Olivia's supposed to be in there. Help me bust it open."

Ghost, Caveman and T-Rex arrived behind Garner. Together, they hit the double doors at the same time.

The locks gave way and the doors flew open.

All five men rushed in.

Garner stopped to render aid to the woman lying on the floor. "It's Mrs. Penders. I've got her. Find Miss Dawson!"

The four men spread out, each taking a different aisle to the back of the store.

Hawkeye made it there first and pushed through the door reading Authorized Personnel Only to the storeroom in the back. "Check behind the boxes!" he yelled to the others, but kept going straight for the back exit, knowing in his gut that they wouldn't find Olivia in the storeroom.

He burst through the back door to the loading dock and ground to a halt, his breathing ragged and his heart so tight in his chest he couldn't breathe.

Black skid marks marred the pavement, indicating a rapid getaway.

Hawkeye leaped to the ground and ran around the side of the building, hoping to catch sight of the vehicle that had left the trail of rubber.

Nothing. The side street and Main Street were empty of all traffic. No cars, trucks or even bicycles moved through the little town.

Olivia was gone.

Chapter Fourteen

The bouncing and jolting motion shook Liv out of the black cloud fogging her brain. She clawed her way to consciousness, knowing in the back of her mind that someone needed help and it was up to her to get it. Her head pounded and bile roiled in her belly.

Cracking open an eyelid, she looked around at what she assumed was the floorboard in the backseat of a four-door, crew-cab truck. The smell of sweat and diesel fuel nearly made her gag. But she fought back the reflex, careful not to make a sound. She stood more of a chance to escape if Sweeney thought she was still unconscious.

Since he'd taken her out the back of the grocery store, no one would know Donald Sweeney had her. Definitely no one had a clue where he was taking her. With a thousand places in the surrounding hills and mountains he could dump her body, she wouldn't be found until some poor hikers stumbled across her bleached bones, picked clean by the numerous scavengers inhabiting the land.

Liv chased away the morbid thoughts, clearing her mind to think of a way out of Sweeney's clutches. If she could get away, she could find her way back home.

The truck bounced along what she assumed was a gravel road until it rolled to a stop.

Sweeney got out, opened the back door of the truck and reached inside for her.

Liv planted her boot in his face as hard as she could.

The ex-marine staggered backward, clutching his nose. "You bitch!" he roared.

Bolting upright, Liv scrambled through the door and fell onto the ground.

Sweeney lunged for her.

Liv tucked her arms close to her side and rolled away. When she was far enough out of his reach, she bunched her knees beneath her and shot to her feet. She ran as fast as she could toward a white house with a wide front porch and nearly fell to her knees when she realized where she was.

Oh, dear Lord, he'd brought her home. If she could get inside, she could lock the doors, grab her father's shotgun and call for help. Then she remembered she'd locked the doors and her purse was somewhere back in the store with the unconscious Mrs. Penders.

She couldn't afford to take the time to locate the spare key and enter the house. Hell, windows wouldn't stop him from getting to her anyway. Her best bet would be to hide. In the barn or in the woods.

The sharp crack of gunfire shocked her into running faster. He was shooting at her! She couldn't move fast enough to get across the open expanses of the pastures to the tree line.

Altering her direction, she ran for the barn. Once inside, she turned and slammed the door shut. Sliding the long bolt home, she slipped the inside lock in place. Then she ran to the door at the other end of the barn and did the same.

The only other entry points were the glass window in the tack room and the sliding barn door in the loft where they dropped hay from above. Without a ladder, Sweeney couldn't get in that way.

Remembering there was an old telephone in the tack room, Liv raced for it. As she reached the open tack-room door, a shot rang out and glass shards scattered across the floor.

No. No. No.

Sweeney had found the window and would make his way inside if she didn't stop him.

Liv dared to peek around the door frame into the tack room.

Sweeney was using the barrel of his pistol to break the rest of the glass out of the window. When he pulled himself up into the gap, Liv ran into the room and jumped up, reaching for the rifle that should have been hanging over the door. It was gone!

That was when she remembered CJ had been the last one to use it. He'd carried it into the house that morning to clean and must have left it there.

Without a weapon, Liv ran back into the barn, grabbed a pitchfork hanging on a nail near a stall. She ran back to the tack room, hoping to catch Sweeney before he could clear his big body through the window.

He had just dropped to the floor when she rounded the corner. The man glared and raised the pistol, aiming at her.

Using the pitchfork as a club, she swung with all of her might, knocking the gun from his hand.

He yelped in pain and fell backward.

Liv jabbed at the man, the tines of the tool piercing Sweeney's leg.

Screaming, he grabbed the implement and yanked it out of her hands and his leg and threw it against the wall.

Liv grabbed the door handle as she ran through the tack-room door and slammed it between them, hoping for enough time to make it out of the barn before he caught up to her.

Stormy whinnied loudly, his distress making Liv's heart hurt. If the bastard started shooting toward the horses, Liv would give herself up to save them. She had to get outside, away from the animals before one of them became collateral damage.

With her hand on the barn-door levers, she heard the tack-room door crash open behind her. It was now or never. She slid the lock to the side and rammed the door open.

Before she could take a step forward, a huge hand clamped down on her shoulder and slammed her to the ground. Her head hit hard and she blacked out.

HAWKEYE STOOD IN the middle of Main Street, shoving his hand through his hair, not knowing which direction to turn, where to look or whom to call for help.

A sheriff's vehicle pulled up in front of him and Sheriff Scott jumped out. "I came as fast as I could."

The loud wail of a siren screamed up the road toward them, heralding the arrival of an ambulance.

Sheriff Scott took Hawkeye's arm and maneuvered him out of the middle of the road.

The emergency medical technicians got out their rescue equipment and converged on Mrs. Penders, who was just coming to when they arrived.

Sheriff Scott pulled Garner aside and demanded, "What happened?"

Hawkeye swung his gaze from one end of Main Street to the other, without any idea as to which way to go. "Someone knocked out Mrs. Penders and took Olivia hostage."

"Did anyone see who it was?" the sheriff asked.

"No. Whoever it was hit Mrs. Penders from behind," Garner said. "Based on the finger-prints you lifted from the spray can and the gasoline jug, it could be one of the two men who vandalized her house last night."

"It's not Eddie Martin," the sheriff said, his face grim. "One of his neighbors found him in a ditch a mile from his house this morning. He's dead."

Hawkeye felt the blood drain from his face. CJ had fired a shot when he saw someone in front of Liv's house. Had the bullet killed his stepfather? "Any idea what killed him?"

"It appears he was bludgeoned to death with a blunt object sometime last night. The coroner will be able to tell us more when he conducts the autopsy." Sheriff Scott clicked the button on his radio and spoke. "Put out an APB on Don Sweeney. He's suspected of assault with a deadly weapon and of abducting Olivia Dawson."

Dispatch acknowledged and sent out the message to other deputies on patrol.

It was a start, but the longer the lead Sweeney had on them, the less likely they would find Olivia before he did something more drastic, like kill her.

Hawkeye refused to accept that as an option. He had to find her, and soon.

"Is there any chance he might use her as

a hostage to negotiate his passage out of the country?" the sheriff asked.

"Given he's a parolee, he knows what will happen if he's caught. He'll end up in jail for the rest of his life." Garner's lips tightened. "Knowing Sweeney, he'll do anything to keep from going back to jail."

Hawkeye balled his fists, wishing he could hit something. "Where would he have taken her?"

"The sheriff is headed out to the Sweeney place."

"And what are we supposed to do in the meantime? He could have taken her anywhere." Hawkeye spun in a circle. "I can't just stand here and do nothing."

"I've mobilized the team. Ghost is going to the feed store to ask questions about Sweeney. I'm sending Caveman and T-Rex out to the area where you two were chased by the men on ATVs. Since we cleared the gang from the res, we figure the men out there last night had to be some of the Free America group."

"They were trying to scare us away from something."

"That's why I have two of the team headed out that way."

"I hope they're heavily armed. The men chasing us fired shots."

"They have rifles and handguns. They'll be looking for the caves you mentioned."

"Do you think Sweeney will take Olivia to one of those caves?" Hawkeye started toward his truck. "I should go with them."

"If you go, and she's not in one of those caves, it would take you too long to get back out of the hills to be of any help in Grizzly Pass. You should stay here in town and wait for word."

"I can't wait. I have to do something."

"Then go to her ranch. I'm sure there are some animals to take care of in her absence."

Hawkeye nodded. CJ would be getting back from his mother's by now and wondering what had happened to them. Maybe he'd have an idea where to look for Olivia.

Hawkeye almost laughed out loud at how useless he felt and how desperate he was to find Olivia. He'd even ask the teen for help.

"I'll go." He held up his cell phone. "I'll have my cell phone on me, but it doesn't work out at her place. Call the ranch number." He gave Garner the number.

Garner laid a hand on his arm. "Miss Dawson will be all right. She's one tough young lady."

"Yeah, she kept saying she could take care of herself." His chest tightened. "But Sweeney is a trained killer."

Hawkeye climbed into his truck and started the engine. He wanted to go out to the caves with the other men on the team. At the same time, he wanted to be with Ghost asking the feed-store owner if he had any idea where Sweeney hung out. But either option might be a waste of time.

Sweeney could disappear into the mountains with Olivia and no one would ever find him. His training in the Marine Corps would make him an expert at blending into the terrain. His only obstacle would be carrying a woman who would fight tooth and nail to get free.

Come on, Olivia. Get away from the bastard and let us know where you are.

He drove out of the parking lot and headed toward Stone Oak Ranch. Where else could he go?

His gaze scanned every side street, searched the nearby hills and looked into every face he passed on his way through town. Did anyone know where Olivia was? He'd just about reached the end of Main Street when his cell phone rang.

Startled by the ringing, he fumbled to hit the talk button without checking the caller ID. "Hawkeye here." He slowed at the end of town before he lost reception.

"Mr. Walsh, it's CJ." The voice on the line was so faint, Hawkeye could barely make out the words.

"CJ, where are you?"

"I'm in Miss Liv's house. You need to get here as soon as possible."

"What's wrong?"

"There's a strange truck in the yard and I heard gunfire and yelling in the barn. I found the spare key and came into the house."

Hawkeye's pulse leaped and he gunned the accelerator. "Stay hidden, CJ. I'm on my way."

"I have the rifle. I could go see what's happening."

"No!" Hawkeye yelled. "Stay away from the barn, CJ. Call 911 and tell them you have an emergency and to send everything they have."

"Mr. Walsh, is Miss Liv with you? I thought I heard her voice in the barn."

Hawkeye didn't want to answer the question,

knowing the teen would want to help his new boss, no matter the cost.

"Please, Mr. Walsh. Tell me Miss Liv is with you," CJ whispered.

Static filled the line and Hawkeye lost reception.

He didn't have time to go back to town and get the sheriff. If CJ did as he was told, he'd notify the sheriff and they'd send help.

In the meantime, he had to get to Olivia before Sweeney killed her, if he hadn't already.

Chapter Fifteen

Liv struggled to the surface of what felt like a deep dark well. When she opened her eyes, she couldn't figure out where she was until she heard Stormy's whickering.

Her head felt like someone had hit it with a sledgehammer again and again, the throbbing so intense she could barely keep her eyes open.

At first she couldn't quite understand why she was in the barn, sitting on the floor, staring at the underside of the stairs to the loft.

When she tried to move her arms, she couldn't. Something anchored her wrists to one of the tall timbers that stretched from the floor to the roof.

Then everything that had happened rushed back at her like a tidal wave of memories, threatening to drown her in its wake.

Sweeney.

Movement around and behind her made her turn her head and wince.

Don Sweeney was pouring something from a jug all over a hay bale against the wall. The pungent scent of gasoline filled Liv's nostrils.

"What are you doing?" she asked, her voice hoarse, fear pinching her vocal cords.

"You're so smart—figure it out." He emptied the jug and flung it behind him. Then he pulled a lighter out of his pocket.

"So that's it? You're going to burn the barn down with me in it?" Liv knew her life was on the line and she would die in the fire, but a sense of calm stole over her. She had to keep her wits about her, if she hoped to get out of this alive. "Why?"

"What's it matter? You'll be as dead as your father in a few minutes." He rolled his thumb on the wheel and a flame lit his face.

"So my father's death wasn't the accident they say it was," she said as calmly as she could. "He didn't fall from his horse."

"Oh, he fell all right. After I hit him in the head."

Liv's stomach roiled and she nearly choked on the bile rising up her throat. "Why?"

"Why? Why? Why?" He faced her, the flame reflected in his eyes. "I'll tell you why. Because once you're labeled, your life is over. You can't get a decent job, you can't make a living and you have to work for idiots like old man Nelson, who couldn't care less that you were once the most decorated sniper in the Corps. All he cared about was how many sacks of feed I could move. That's why!" He flung the lighter at the hay bale and watched as the little flame lit the gasoline. Like a live organism, it raced around the interior of the barn, feeding on the fuel like a starving beast.

Stormy screamed and kicked at the walls of his stall.

"I did it for the money."

"You killed an innocent man for money?"

"Hell yeah. And if you hadn't decided to stay on your ranch, I would have gotten away with it."

"You would have gotten away with it if you'd left me alone."

He coughed and sneered at her. "You should have just stayed away. Now they'll know it was me." He snorted. "But I don't plan on sticking around to face any music." He ran for the door.

"Sweeney!" Liv cried out. "Who paid you?"

"Someone with a whole lot more money than you and I have. And it'll get me the hell out of this country. Say hello to your father when you get where you're going." He flung open the barn door and ran outside.

The sharp report of gunfire sounded out in the barnyard.

Sweeney roared, cursing loud enough Liv could hear him over the crackle of the flames.

The smoke grew thicker.

She struggled to loosen the ropes binding her wrists, but they were so tight, she couldn't get her hands through. Instead, she rubbed the ropes on the edges of the six-by-six post, hoping to fray the strands. At the rate she was going and the smoke was building, she'd die of smoke inhalation before she worked herself free.

Then she heard the sound of a younger voice cry out. "Let go of me!"

CJ.

Liv struggled harder to get free. CJ was in trouble. The ex-marine would show no mercy toward the boy.

"You little brat!" Sweeney cursed.

"Leave Miss Liv alone!" CJ yelled.

Something hit the side of the barn, and the

next thing Liv knew, CJ's limp body was thrown through the door. He landed like a rag doll and lay still. The barn door closed, shutting them inside with the fire and smoke.

"CJ!" Liv yelled, sucked in a lungful of smoke and shouted. "CJ!"

HAWKEYE STOOD ON the accelerator the entire three miles along the highway to the Stone Oak Ranch. The truck nearly went off the road on several of the curves, but he refused to lose control. By the time he reached the gate, his heart was racing and his lungs were so tight he could barely breathe.

Smoke rose over the top of the trees ahead.

What hell was this? Had Sweeney brought her out to her ranch to torch her home with her inside it?

He steered the truck along the winding driveway, cursing the trees in the way of his view. When he burst out into the open in front of the house, his heart stopped.

Smoke billowed up from the barn. A truck spun in the barnyard and headed directly for him.

Hawkeye slammed his foot to the accelerator and drove straight at the other vehicle. Anticipating that Sweeney would try to dodge him and keep going, Hawkeye braced himself, slammed on his brakes and twisted the steering wheel sharply to the left. The back end of the truck skidded sideways just as Sweeney's truck swung to the right.

Sweeney crashed into the bed of Hawkeye's truck, pushing him back around straight.

For a brief moment, Sweeney's truck didn't move.

Hawkeye shifted into Reverse and slammed into the passenger side of Sweeney's truck and pushed the vehicle sideways, crushing it between his tailgate and a tree. All four doors of the truck were blocked by either the tree or Hawkeye's truck.

With Sweeney trapped inside, Hawkeye hopped out of the cab and ran for the barn.

Flames leaped from the roof and the horses inside screamed.

Hawkeye pulled on the barn door, but it wouldn't open. He braced his foot beside the door and pulled as hard as he could. The door budged a little and then flew open.

Smoke billowed out, catching him full in the face.

His eyes stung and he coughed. Pulling his

T-shirt up over his mouth and nose, he ducked low and charged into the barn. "Olivia!"

"Hawkeye?" she called out, her weak voice hoarse, almost unrecognizable. She coughed.

Hawkeye tripped over something on the floor.

"Get CJ out," Olivia said and coughed again.

He stared down at what he had mistaken for a pile of rags. The teen lay in a crumpled heap on the ground.

Hawkeye scooped him up in his arms and carried him out of the barn and several yards away from the building before he laid him on the ground.

Without hesitation, Hawkeye dived back into the barn. The smoke was thicker. He crawled along the floor, searching for Olivia.

"Talk to me!" he yelled.

"Get the horses out," she said.

"Not until I get you out."

"You can't. Please, save the horses."

Hawkeye ignored her pleas and followed the sound of her voice to the space beneath the stairs.

Olivia sat with her back to a post, her arms behind her. "It's no use. You can't untie me fast enough." She coughed, the sound weak and pathetic. Then her head drooped and she passed out.

Hawkeye felt behind her, found the rope securing her to the post. He dug in his pocket for his knife, pulled it out and sawed on the ropes until they broke free.

His lungs burned and he could barely see through his stinging eyes, but he refused to leave Liv there to die.

Once he had her free, he dragged her across the floor and out of the barn, where he collapsed on the ground beside her.

Vehicles pulled into the barnyard, sirens blaring and lights flashing all around him.

T-Rex, Ghost, Caveman and Garner rushed forward with the sheriff and his deputies.

"Horses," Hawkeye said. "Four of them."

"It's too dangerous," the sheriff said.

"To hell with that." Ghost ran for the barn, followed by the other men of Garner's team.

Moments later, they led the four horses out of the burning barn and into the fresh mountain air.

Emergency medical technicians surrounded CJ, Olivia and Hawkeye.

They fixed oxygen masks to Olivia and CJ.

When they tried to put one on Hawkeye, he pushed them away. "I'm okay."

"Smoke inhalation isn't something to ignore," Garner said.

"I'm going with these two to the hospital."

"Okay, but let the medical staff take care of you, too. I need you back on the team ASAP."

Hawkeye nodded. "I'll be there. Did they get Sweeney?"

Garner nodded. "Yeah, but he's in bad shape. He's unconscious right now and not responding."

"I hope that bastard dies," Hawkeye said through gritted teeth.

"Yeah, I do, too. But not before he tells us who he's working for."

At the moment, Hawkeye didn't care about anything or anyone but Olivia and CJ. If they lived, he'd be all right with the world and get on with the job of finding the people responsible for all of the problems in the area.

WHEN LIV WOKE AGAIN, she stared up at the white ceiling and wondered where she was. The strong scent of disinfectant filled the air and the sound of an intercom calling for a doctor grounded her. She was in the hospital.

"Hey," a voice said beside her.

She turned to find Hawkeye sitting in the chair next to her hospital bed. "What happened?" she asked, her voice sounding more like that of a bullfrog than a woman.

"I'm sorry, but they weren't able to save your barn."

"The barn?" Her eyes widened. "CJ?"

"He's going to be okay. Mild concussion and smoke inhalation, but he'll be back to work in no time."

"The horses?" Liv asked.

"The guys got all four out of the barn. They're in the pasture with the rest of your herd."

Liv relaxed against the pillow and closed her eyes. "What about you?"

He lifted her hand and pressed it to his cheek. "I've never been more scared in my life."

She chuckled and coughed. "You?" Liv opened her eyes and looked at him. "Scared? Why?"

"When I couldn't find you in the barn, I thought... Hell...I don't know what I thought." He squeezed her hand. "But I wasn't coming out without you."

Liv drew his hand to her lips and pressed a kiss to his knuckles. "You could have died."

His eyes welled and he shook his head. "I couldn't live with myself if I didn't save you."

She shook her head. "Hawkeye, you can't save everyone."

"No. But I had to try." He smiled. "I have goals."

"Goals?"

"Yeah. I want to give civilian life a shot."

Liv frowned. "What do you mean? I thought you loved being a part of the military?"

"I do, but I want more. I think I could be a pretty good ranch hand for a certain ranch owner." He sat up straighter and puffed out his chest. "I've got experience."

Liv's heart swelled. "Will you ride horses?"

He brushed his lips across hers in a light kiss. "I'll ride anything she wants me to ride, if she'll give me a chance."

"I don't know," Liv said, shaking her head, when what she really wanted to do was shout with joy. "It sounds a lot like commitment to me. And I'm not so sure you and I are ready for commitment."

"Maybe we aren't, but I'd like to give it a shot." He touched his lips to her forehead and the tip of her nose. "And I could do contract work for the DHS to bring in additional income."

Liv sighed. "Hmm. Sounds like you have it all figured out." She lay back, feeling more relaxed and satisfied than she'd felt since coming back to Grizzly Pass. "I think I could use a guy like you on the ranch."

"I hope so, because I think I could fall for a boss like you."

Her eyes widened. She'd felt their connection from the first day. She'd known he could be the one. But hearing him say he could fall for her made her world light up. Despite the raspiness in her throat and the pain it caused her to talk, she had to ask. "We've only just met. How do you know?"

"Darlin', when you know, you know." Then he kissed her and proved he wasn't just fooling around.

They might not have all the answers to why someone would want Liv and her father dead. They hadn't solved the mystery of what was going on in Grizzly Pass, but they had found the answer to the most important question of all. How do you know?

* * * * *

Check out the previous books in the
BALLISTIC COWBOYS *series:*

HOT COMBAT
HOT TARGET

And don't miss the final book

HOT RESOLVE

Available soon from Harlequin Intrigue!

Get 2 Free Books,
Plus 2 Free Gifts—
just for trying the Reader Service!

HARLEQUIN *Presents*®

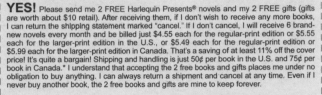

Get 2 Free Books,
Plus 2 Free Gifts —
just for trying the
Reader Service!

Get 2 Free Books,
Plus 2 Free Gifts—
just for trying the Reader Service!

HARLEQUIN *super romance*